# Voices from a Drum
## Earl G. Long

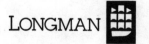

LONGMAN

Longman Group Limited,
Edinburgh Gate, Harlow,
Essex CM20 2JE, England
and Associated Companies throughout the world

Carlong Publishers (Caribbean) Limited
PO Box 489
Kingston 10

33 Second Street
Newport West
Kingston 13, Jamaica

Longman Trinidad Limited
Boundary Road
San Juan
Trinidad

Copp Clark Longman Ltd.
2775 Matheson Blvd East
Mississauga
Ontario L4W 4P7
Canada

Longman Publishing Group
10 Bank Street
White Plains
New York 10601–1951, USA

First published 1996

**British Library Cataloguing in Publication Data**
A CIP record for this book is available from the British Library

**Series Editor**
Stewart Brown

Set in Baskerville

Produced through Longman Malaysia, PP

ISBN 0 582 28709. X

# Dedication and Acknowledgement

This book is dedicated to the memory of the grand heroes and story tellers of my childhood: Ezra Long, Harry Simmons, Hilton and Anelta Tobière, Wellington and Flavie Jacob.

My thanks to Ossie Davis and Ed Layne for unrelenting encouragement; to Rosalind Ward for getting things done; and to my editor John Bates for much help.

# Contents

# Prologue

On the western coast of the island, the hills rise immediately from the Caribbean Sea without the interruption of beaches. The people who live in those hills have anchored their small houses to the steep hillsides with poles cut from the trees that grow around them. Their villages have names like Latanier, Amande, Mahôt and Laurier, that are also the names of the trees of the montane forests.

One village bears a different name; it is called Tambour – which means drum – and sits where the air is colder, higher than the other villages. When the clouds are lowered by rain, and for much of the wet season, Tambour disappears from view, along with the hilltops.

The best drummers on the island come from Tambour. The people of Latanier, and Mahôt and other neighbouring villages say that is because the drums of Tambour are covered with human skin. Sometimes, someone from the city, emboldened by rum and the nearness of his companions, will ask a villager from Tambour whether the legend is true; and the villager will smile and shrug, leaving the questioner no wiser, but unwilling to persist.

Part One

# Voices from a Drum

*Earl G Long*

## Chapter 1

# The mabouya

For generations, the warriors of Mabouya's tribe had hunted and killed the tall black people and the pale men who brought them to the island. But one day, the sea brought a black fugitive to the village of Manatee – his feeble efforts with a broken oar were too weak to keep his rotten canoe from the push of the waves. The Caribs rushed to the shore, taunting the parched, naked man; daring him to land, and laughing when the children's stones hit him. Two men dragged him ashore when his canoe foundered, and hurried him to the chief's hut. On his knees, he pleaded with urgent signs that they let him beat an old drum that was lying near a hut, before they killed him. None of the villagers said anything, but the chief sensed their amused curiosity and nodded despite the shaman's frown. The boy Mabouya saw that the stocky, muscular man stopped trembling as he reached for the drum and began caressing it like and old friend. He listened transfixed as the drummer's large, thick hands tapped the drum skin, and he began to sing.

The small drum answered, first with a plaintive 'Mmmm ... mmmm ... mmmm,' then louder and louder, until their village was wrapped around with the noise of great winds roaring like the storm god *Houracan* in his annual fury; from hot dry plains, across savannahs that spread wider than their sea, and through massive steaming forests, came the wretched pleas for lost children. Mabouya thought that he could see, at the edge of the village clearing, dark shapes that were men, no ... women, no ... children, giants tall as two men, no ... dwarfs. The shapes would turn to the drum, leap forward with arms outstretched – but move no closer – their mouths open as if screaming 'Here! Over here!'

The women of the Mabouya's village cried for the sons and husbands who had never come back from the sea; the men cried for the wives and daughters who had died screaming as they struggled to give birth to children who would die too. They saw the drummer's loneliness stretched precariously across unbroken oceans, reaching for a place to stop – any place, a rock or even a stone.

They let the drummer live.

One day, after Nzo had learned their language, Mapipi, the chief, called him to his hut, and sent for the ten-year-old Mabouya. 'Teach the boy,' Mapipi said.

The Caribs called Nzo, 'Entahso'. They let him help with collecting whelks and sea urchins from the reefs, and preparing manioc flour; then forgot he was not one of them. Mapipi forbade him and Mabouya to go to sea, even in the large canoes with six rowers. Once, Entahso asked his Mabouya why.

'After a very bad storm, there was a lot of rain, and the river was carrying down trees it had torn away from the forest. I saw an *iouana* holding on to a large branch, so I jumped in and climbed on the branch to get it. I was only as high as your navel. But I didn't hold it near enough the head, so it turned and bit me. I let go of the branch and the river carried me away ... all the way to the sea. Some men jumped into a canoe and they pulled me out. They say I wasn't breathing, but I was still holding on to the *iouana*. After that, they called me 'Mabouya,' like the little black and white lizard under the stones that sticks to your skin and never lets go until you burn it. The chief says I can hunt agouti and *manicou*. I can go into the forest, but not the sea. The sea remembers my face; if it sees me again, I will drown. That is why.'

Entahso nodded; he felt no great interest in lizards that lay under rocks, but he rejoiced silently at what he had learned about the boy's determination. He who had been the chief drummer of the Pende, feared even by the drummers of the Kongo, Bandundu and Kasai, resolved to live forever in the Carib boy. For centuries to come, long after the tribe was forgotten, his hands would beat drums, and he would continue to sing the old songs of death and rejoicing and birth. His fame would spread around the island, as it had done along the Congo river, from Matadi to Kasongo. He laughed out loud and enjoyed the sound of his laughter – for the first time since the slavers had taken him away.

Every evening, as soon as the winds from the hills began blowing the day's heat out to sea, Entahso would bring the drums they had made out of his hut. Then he would set Mabouya to work, learning new rhythms, and chanting songs in six languages, some of them sacred languages that were known only by the master drummers. He taught Mabouya the songs for special occasions, and those that could be sung for just the joy of singing. The most intense and frightening lessons were learning to speak the language of the drum. Then Entahso's eyes would roll upwards until only the whites showed, and sweat would pour off him as if small storms were breaking over his head. At these times the villagers would move away and shiver, as Entahso's hands made the the drum speak with the voices of waterfalls and storms and thunder. Sometimes they heard sounds that they said were like the mountains speaking to each other, or like immense rocks rolling down hillsides and over each other.

Mabouya's hands hardened, like his teacher's, until the skin of his palms grew thick like horn, and he could no longer close his palms tightly. But each time he thought he had learned all Entahso had to teach, the other would say, 'Good, now we can begin the next song.' It was three years before Entahso finally said, 'Ah! now you are beginning to learn.' A year later, he said, 'You must now make your own drum. A great drum. One that you will use when all of us are dead.'

'But I will be dead too,' Mabouya smiled.

Entahso looked past him. 'You will be the Master Drummer,' he said.

'What?' Mabouya asked.

'Chief of the drums,' Entahso said simply.

One day, at the height of the dry season, Entahso asked the chief's permission to find a tree suitable for making Mabouya's great drum. Mapipi sent for the canoe-makers. Yes, they could help cut down and transport the trunk of a *gomier* tree, whose wood would not crack when it dried – it was the same that they used for their canoes. It took three men one whole day to cut down the tree with their stone axes, and two more men to roll the trunk section to the sea and tow it by canoe to Manatee.

Entahso hollowed out the trunk by burning it out carefully and slowly; then Mabouya scraped away the charred wood with conch-shell knives until he could rub his palm against the wall and not feel any splinters. When that was done, Entahso stood the cylinder upright and walked around it slowly. Sometimes, he sat and stared at it without moving for so long that the children would compete with each other at trying to make him look away. One day he called to Mabouya, 'Come look at the drum. Tell me what you see. It is your drum. I cannot put the things I see on it.'

So Mabouya sat and looked at the drum, but the children teased him so much that he said to Entahso, 'I see myself beating the children on their heads with a heavy stick.'

Entahso persisted. 'Look at the drum.'

So the gecko clung to his task and slowly began to see the long, gaunt faces of death; the fat, laughing faces of celebration; saw people of different colours with strange noses and mouths; saw fish as large as the hills and animals as tall as three huts and snakes as long as two war canoes.

He told Entahso of his visions, and the village children stopped their games to crowd closer to see those things too. Entahso handed Mabouya a piece of charcoal. 'Mark them on the drum,' he said.

When Mabouya had covered the surface of the drum with outlines of his visions, the children ran to call their parents, and the parents called the the chief and Kilibri, the shaman. 'Where do these things come from?' Kilibri asked. 'They are not in the forests here or in the sea or in the ground. How can Mabouya see them?'

'I have seen them in my country,' Entahso replied, 'but I did not tell Mabouya. The drum told him.'

The shaman looked at Mapipi; the chief stared back perplexed. The men shook their heads; the women told the children not to look at the drum or the creatures would come for them in their dreams.

'Now we must carve these things into the wood,' Entahso said to Mabouya when the curious had moved away. 'But we have only stone and shell. We must get iron axes and knives. We shall have to steal them from the white strangers ... in the north. And we need a goatskin for the drum.'

'What is a goat?' Mabouya asked.

'It's an animal about this high,' and he pointed to his knee. 'It has two little spears on its head, and it eats grass. Its feet are like an agouti's.'

'We cannot use an agouti?' Mabouya asked.

'Too small,' Entahso explained.

'And the strangers have goats?' Mabouya assumed.

'Yes,' Entahso answered.

'The chief will say no,' Mabouya warned.

'Then we will go in secret,' Entahso said.

In the end, Mabouya persuaded Entahso to ask Mapipi for permission to search for forest plants with which to stain the drum.

'How long will you take?' Mapipi asked.

'Two days . . . three days,' Entahso said casually.

Mapipi frowned uncertainly. 'Do you want a warrior to come with you?'

'No,' said Entahso, 'we will not go far from the forests in the hills.' And he pointed to the east.

'Do not go to the north. The strangers are moving south . . . one day there will be war. Go tomorrow,' Mapipi said, and dismissed them by turning back to honing the edge of an ornate shell knife.

The next day, the two rubbed their bodies with red *annatto* dye for protection against insects, and set out with smoked *manicou* meat and roasted manioc flour in pouches of woven grass. Mabouya carried a bow and a quiver of poison-tipped arrows. Entahso carried a stone axe and two javelins with fire-hardened points. The sense of adventure and guilt pushed them hurriedly into the hills. When they reached the thick, fragrant rainforests near the clouds, safe from any spies sent after them, they turned left and headed north. Mabouya walked ahead, pushing a path for them through an unbroken wall of vines, ferns and mosses. Entahso watched the ground carefully, wary of the *mapipi*, the short-tempered pit viper – the chief's namesake – that would lie camouflaged among the leaves on the forest floor waiting for prey. They stopped for rest when the sun was in the middle of the sky, and its light illuminated even the crevices among the buttress roots of the forest trees. After drinking from a stream, they waded out to some large rocks where they could sit and soak their feet in the cool water. Mabouya turned to his companion.

'Entahso, why have you not taken a wife? Do you not like our women?'

'The drum is my wife,' Entahso replied.

Mabouya laughed, 'The drum cannot satisfy your needs. It cannot bring you water. It cannot give you children. Tell me why you have not asked Mapipi for a woman. Maybe he can find a woman for you in another clan.'

'Mapipi spared my life so that I could teach you the drum. If I take a wife, I may have a son. Then I shall want to teach him the drum. But there can be only one master drummer. A long time ago, my parents sent me to the chief drummer of my village to become his son. His own sons did not want to learn the drum . . . they wanted to be warriors. They died . . . I am alive.'

Mabouya stared into the stream while he pondered silently on his teacher's revelations; and Entahso was bending to collect some water to moisten a handful of manioc flour on a heliconia leaf when Mabouya called out suddenly, '*Zodomeh . . . zodomeh!*'

Entahso looked to where Mabouya was pointing, just in time to see a black shape almost as long as his arm, flow like the water itself, to hide beneath a small overhang at the bank of the stream. Mabouya rushed into the forest and came back with a cut section of a vine which he began pounding with a small rock.

'Go down the stream and wait. Grab at it when it comes to you and throw it quickly to the bank . . . it is too slippery to hold.'

Then he crept quietly to the place where the fish had disappeared, and began squeezing the crushed vine in the water just upstream of its hiding place. A milky sap diffused into the water, and flowed past the hiding place of the *zodomeh*; a few moments later the fish emerged gasping as if overcome by a sudden, desperate thirst. The current took it towards Entahso, who was squatting between two rocks where the stream was channelled. With a great flourish, he scooped the fish so far out of the water that it took them several minutes to find it in the thick underbrush.

Later, when the flesh had been sucked off every bone, and Entahso had been able for a brief time to forget his craving for roasted goat and boiled *macambo*, Mabouya asked about the strange animals he had seen in his vision. He nodded solemnly as Entahso described antelope bearing straight and curved spears, moving in uncountable numbers across plains on which there were no mountains and no hills. Entahso described cats large enough to eat a man; giraffes so tall that they could look down on the chief's hut; and hippopotamuses larger and longer than war canoes. But when he described an animal that was heavier than all the men in Manatee put together, with a nose like a snake, and with legs like tree trunks, Mabouya collapsed in laughter, saying that he had seen such animals in his vision, but they could not weigh more than five men. He held up one hand with fingers outstretched. 'No more than that,' he said with satisfaction, and shook his head in amusement at Entahso's exaggeration. 'Now, we must hurry,' he urged shortly. 'We should begin seeing the smoke from the strangers' camps tomorrow afternoon ... after we have climbed two more hills. I have heard the warriors telling Mapipi where they have seen campfires and new clearings in the forest.'

But when they had reached the summit of the first hill and looked across the valley to the hill they were to climb the next day, they saw the shelter, the small pen with chickens and the tethered goats of an invader's camp.

'We will camp here tonight,' Mabouya said angrily. 'They should not be here ... they should not be coming into our lands.'

## Chapter 2

# Voice of the earthshaker

Entahso looked down at the rough hut and regretted his decision to seek the skin of a goat for Mabouya's drum. Old, searing memories rushed back, clanging like hot neck and leg irons, and he said no more as they lay down for the night, but he lay awake and trembled until the next morning. When it was time to move down to spy on the camp, his fear had given way to anger at the strangers for his past captivity and his present tiredness. He was middle-aged now, and uncertain about how much help he could be to Mabouya if it came to fighting. He hoped the settlers did not have guns.

As soon as they had washed the sleep from their faces, they rubbed their bodies with more *annatto* paste, and Mabouya rubbed powdered charcoal over his face. They crept through the underbrush, stopping to listen for strange sounds. On the flat valley floor they were unable to see the camp but used the sun to guide them. At the edge of the clearing, they lay in the grass for an hour gazing at the hut, enduring the explorations and stings of flies and ants. Eventually, a tall, muscular man emerged and went into some nearby bushes. When he emerged, a younger man followed suit. They then started a fire in a mud hearth and breakfasted on something they roasted. The older man walked to the back of the hut and reappeared upon a horse. At the sight of the large animal with the man astride it, Mabouya started violently and would have run back into the forest if Entahso had not held him down. 'The animal will not harm us,' he said, 'but the man can now move very quickly. We must wait until he has gone far away.'

Mabouya lay quietly, his mouth agape with disbelief at the grotesque, impossible apparition.

The horse and rider moved towards the mouth of the valley, and Mabouya laid out his plan. He would move to hide at the side of the hut; Entahso would move towards the door but remain hidden in the brush. Then he was to call out as if in greeting. When the young man emerged, Mabouya would kill him with a blow to the head with his axe. They moved out, and when Entahso had crept within earshot of the hut he called out, '*Aïee!*'

The man came out of the hut. '*Papa?*' he answered, peering about, then turned to his left just as Mabouya lunged at him. But the man was quick; he dodged the blow and struck out hard, catching Mabouya on the side of the head. Before the Carib could recover, the settler had thrown him to the ground and pinned him with his knees. He was reaching for the stone axe when Entahso rushed out of the bushes, a javelin held aloft. The man released Mabouya and ran in the direction the older man had taken, shouting in French as he ran.

'Papa! Papa! Help me!'

His pursuers were gaining on him when the ground shook with the sound of a galloping horse. Mabouya and Entahso froze as the rider, with his machete raised, bore down to them. Take the runaway! I'll kill the savage!' he called.

'Run!' Entahso screamed at Mabouya, as terror loosened his bowels. Mabouya was rooted to the ground, his axe held loosely at his side as he waited to die. Even then, they heard the 'Fweet ... fweet ... fweet!' and saw the arrows as they suddenly attached themselves to the eyes and throat of the two pursuers. As the wounded men fell screaming, two shapes arose from the ground and buried their axes in the heads of the Frenchmen.

Mabouya and Entahso sat on the ground, staring in disbelief at their rescuers who, streaked with camouflaging *annatto* and charcoal, had been invisible while they had lain still in the brush.

'Mapipi told us to follow you,' Taza explained.

Coulirou nodded, 'It does not take three days to collect herbs in the forest.'

'Mapipi is wiser than all of us,' Mabouya said, and turning to Entahso, he asked, 'Will the drum let me carve a *taza* and a *coulirou* on it?'

Entahso nodded, 'It will.'

Mabouya faced Taza. 'Mapipi is angry,' he said with certainty.

'Mapipi is angry,' Taza agreed, then turned to point to the hut, the bodies on the ground and the pen. 'All of this ... we will burn all of this.'

They killed and butchered the chickens and goats, cut up the meat for transportation, and threw the refuse into the hut; the horse had disappeared into the forest. Coulirou gathered up all the iron implements he could find. Then, as if by prearranged agreement with Taza, he went to the body of the older man and made a circular cut around the body at the upper part of the torso. He made a similar cut below the abdomen; then, turning the body on its back, he made a straight cut down the chest. With the man's own knife, he cut away the rectangular strip of skin, and rolled up the bloody trophy. 'This is the skin for your drum,' he said, handing the skin to Mabouya.

They threw the two corpses into the hut, covered them with dry brush, and with embers from the hearth, set the hut on fire.

'We will leave now. We will be in Manatee before the sun sets tomorrow,' Taza said.

The sun had just touched the horizon of the bay when they arrived. The villagers looked away from them as if the adventurers had already ceased to exist. Mabouya's parents remained in their hut. Taza ordered the pair to sit on the ground facing the doorway of Mapipi's hut, and Coulirou squatted behind them. Taza then went into the chief's hut to announce their return. It was almost dark when Mapipi emerged with Kilibri and six clan elders. The chief looked over their heads as if to gather his words from the distance before speaking.

'Entahso, we spared your life because you spoke the language of the forests and the sea and the hills. Entahso, we have let you eat and sleep with us. Entahso, we have made you Mabouya's teacher. Entahso, you have disobeyed the chief of this clan.

'Mabouya, we pulled you from the throat of the sea as it swallowed you. Mabouya, we told you to learn the drum so that you could speak to the earth, like Entahso. Mabouya, you have disobeyed the chief of the clan.

'When a person of the clan disobeys the chief, he tells the clan he is greater than the chief. No one here is greater than Mapipi. Not you, Entahso. Not you, Mabouya. If you were greater than I, you would have to kill me. But I am greater than you, so I should kill you. But because of you, we have discovered and killed two invaders on our land, and we have good trophies. Entahso, you are a foolish old man. Mabouya, you are a foolish boy. I, Mapipi, will not kill you today, but if you are sleeping and I ask you to wake, and you do not; if you are breathing and I ask you to stop, and you do not; if you are swallowing or pissing or shitting and I ask you to stop, and you do not; then I shall take you to the top of the cliffs and break your legs and throw you into the sea. And you will use your hands to keep your eyes out of the water long enough to see the sharks that will fill their bellies with your flesh. Tomorrow, you will prepare the skin for the drum. That is all I have to say.'

With this he rose, dismissed the elders and entered his hut. Coulirou kicked Mabouya and Entahso in the back. 'Go!' he ordered.

Their recent ordeal had made their hunger irrelevant, but Mabouya's mother insisted that they eat a little broth of fish and beans thickened with ground maize.

The next day, they stretched the skin out with pegs hammered into the ground, scraped the underside free of blood and tissue, covered it with salt, and left it to dry in the sun. Two days later, Entahso washed it clean in a stream and stretched it out again. While they waited for the skin to stretch and dry, Mabouya began to carve his vision figures, using the knives they had obtained from the invaders. As he cut the broad outlines into the wood, Entahso would follow and incise the small details of teeth and claws and horns. It was two months before Entahso was satisfied enough to stretch the skin over the drum and secure it with pegs and a harness of rope. Then they painted it with *annatto* and dyes from the forest plants, and outlined the animals in charcoal. Finally, Entahso said, 'It is finished. I shall go and tell Mapipi.'

The entire village assembled with the chief to view the great drum with its fantastic figures and grey, hairless skin. Entahso – at Mabouya's urging – asked Kilibri to bless the drum, and the audience stood and sat and fidgeted for a long time while the shaman placed, with admirable precision, small assemblages of bones, sticks and shells in a circle around the drum and sang sacred, unintelligible incantations. Finally, he sprinkled powders of various colours on the drum while he danced with a weightiness and solemnity that was quite unlike his namesake, the hummingbird. Only when he paused to recover his breath, and caught the chief's eye, did he discover that he had come to the end of the ceremony. Mapipi nodded to Entahso, who looked at Mabouya. 'Your drum is waiting for you,' Entahso said.

Mabouya walked to the drum as slowly as he could without standing still, and tapped the skin with the fingertips of his right hand. At this, the drum answered with a cutting, keening scream that sent the village dogs howling into the bushes and children screaming to their mothers. The listeners ground their teeth gently to ensure they had not been shattered in their mouths. Then Mabouya held his hands high and brought them down hard. And the ground shook as if a monstrous fist had beaten down on it with the glad abandon of long-wanted freedom. The blackbirds and finches around the village fled into the forest, and the older villagers who had stayed in their huts said later that water had jumped out of the clay pots. The sound rolled across the bay, rebounding from cliff to cliff, until no one could tell whether it came from the drum or the earth.

Sometimes, at later festivities, the night wind would carry the sound of the drum to other villages along the coast, and children would look up at the sky for the lightning and see only stars. Inevitably, the people of Mapipi's clan boasted of their drum, and its fame spread along the coast to the other Carib villages and into the hills to the black people and, finally, to their white captors.

The Europeans heard more of the legend as they moved south, destroying villages and crops, killing even dogs and tame parrots, and sparing only the young women whom they used for sport until the women died of hunger and bleeding. Before razing a village, the settlers would search each hut for the drum – reputed to be as high as a man and as wide as his arm-span – wanting it as a trophy to surpass a rival's larger collection of scalps.

Mapipi ordered Mabouya and Entahso to take the drum into the hills. 'Soon, there will be no more Caribs because we are a hard people. And if we cannot chase the invaders away, then we will die. We have never lived with another people. Not with the Ciboneys, not with the Arawaks. And we will not live with the whites, and not with the blacks. Entahso, the people of Manatee give you back the drum. Mabouya, take care of the drum for Entahso's people. That is all I have to say. Now go.'

They forced themselves not to look back as the chief and his warriors burned the village and canoes, shattered every pot, fouled the gardens; then went into battle. The women, old people and children threw their clothes and ornaments into the fires, then climbed the high cliffs to jump into the sea and onto the rocks below.

*Chapter 3*

# Dioub

For two days, the Carib and the African walked westward through the forest-covered hills, stopping only to drink, and to sleep when darkness hid the ground. On the second morning, they awoke to a sudden, imperative cough and the acrid smell of sweat and mildewed clothes. They found themselves in the middle of a circle of black men armed with spears, machetes, and one musket.

'You must have been very tired ... you did not hear us. We became impatient waiting for you to wake,' said one of the men in halting French to Entahso. He towered fully a shoulder above the rest of his company, and was so thin and hard that he seemed to be carved of black *balata* wood.

Mabouya reached quickly for the machete the white settler had once raised to kill him, but it was not at his side. Another of the men held it up, smiling. 'We have your arms,' the first speaker warned. 'If you are a runaway, what are you doing with a Carib? They kill us too.'

'My name is Nzo; the Caribs called me Entahso. I ran away from a plantation in the north called Maravelle. I lived with the Caribs for five years. They let me live with them to teach him ...' Entahso turned towards Mabouya. 'I taught him the drum. The drum! Where is the drum?' he asked in consternation.

'The drum is safe. Why is the Carib with you?' the leader persisted.

'The whites were coming to our village. So the chief told us to take the drum to the hills. Then he burned down the village and went to fight. The women and old people and children must have killed themselves or the invaders must have killed them by now. He is the last of this clan. The drum is not a Carib drum ... it is a sacred Pende drum. But its master is the Carib. His name is Mabouya,' Entahso answered.

16

'A Carib drummer of African drums!' a voice sneered, '*Merde*! Let's kill the Carib and take the drum. The runaway can come with us if he wants.'

'I promised to look after the boy. If you kill him, you will have to kill me too.' Entahso said tiredly. Perhaps that was best, he thought: he owed the Caribs a life.

'Wait! Wait!' the leader said impatiently. 'We are not going to do the slavers' work for them. Nzo, you can come with us ... and the Carib too. But watch him, if he tries to fight one of us, we will kill him. My name is François. Most of us are *marrons* from a plantation called Principale.'

Entahso thought immediately that François's face reminded him of a hatchet. All his features were sharp as if to cut through the wind. His eyes were brighter than they should have been in the soft light of the forest, and were focused on things beyond the trees and the men present.

François looked at Mabouya with new interest. 'Ah-ah! A Carib drummer. This, one must see. Tell me, Mabouya, can you fight as well as you play the drum? If you *can* play the drum.'

Mabouya turned to Entahso for an explanation. Entahso answered, 'The boy is a Carib. So how can he not know how to fight?' Then he translated for Mabouya.

Mabouya grinned. François did not raise the matter again. François turned to one of his group, 'Sivien, give the Carib his machete, and somebody go and get the drum.'

'You seem to know the forest well,' said Entahso. 'How long have you been maroons?'

'Ten months ... I think ... by the moon. Or maybe a year,' François replied, 'but we do not count days any longer. It is more important to find food. There are some other groups ... but most will die in the forest. They eat fruits that make them sick or kill them. If they go down to the coast, the Caribs kill them. We get some food when we raid the plantations, but that is getting harder. The settlers have dogs, and they have begun hunting us.'

'Where are you going? And what will you do with Mabouya and me?' Entahso asked.

'We are going up into the hills in the west. We have heard from other maroons that the hills are too steep for attackers to move through easily. Perhaps we can start small settlements

17

there. It's either that or go back to the plantations . . . and die from torture. And I have something else to do . . .' François added cryptically. 'The Carib: he can help us find food, and hunt. And we need fighters,' François smiled, 'Also it is many years since we heard the drum. Yes, we will want to hear it again.'

With that, François took the food that Entahso and Mabouya carried, and portioned it out as breakfast for the group. Afterwards, the men washed their hands and faces in a nearby stream, then turned away from the sun to walk towards the tall hills.

The newcomers found themselves in the middle of a small, silent column of emaciated and filthy men too tired to contemplate the pains of exhaustion and disease. Entahso and Mabouya tried to fall back so they would not be suffocated by the smell of rot that steamed from the maroons, but Sivien insisted that they remain where he could keep an eye on them.

Occasionally, some of the men would break off pieces of dry resin from incense trees that they passed, and for hours would hold these close to their noses and inhale deeply, their eyes closed in quiet pleasure. Entahso and Mabouya thought the maroons did it because of the newness of the smell, different from anything else in the forest. Then they tried it and understood: the smell was an immediate contact with other times and other places. For a short time, they forgot the agony that lingered from spines embedded in their arms after brushing against small palm trees hairy with black thorns, or from the stinging ants that fell from the leaves into their hair and clothes.

The column could move only slowly, sometimes having to retrace their route because of impassable gorges and cliffs long cut by the forest streams. On one of their frequent rest stops, Mabouya nudged Entahso, and pointed to one of the maroons who had just pushed out a loose tooth with his tongue. 'These men should eat *macoudja* fruit. Their mouths are bleeding,' he said.

Entahso nodded, and spoke to François. 'How do we know the fruit is not poisonous?' François asked.

'Because I'm not dead yet,' Entahso answered impatiently.

François nodded and agreed that they would eat the fruit if Mabouya would help them find it. Three days later, Sivien said to Entahso, 'Thank the Carib for telling us about the fruit. I think I was going to die.'

18

Two weeks later, they stood on a hilltop, and through the trees they could see the dark blue spread of water that was calmer than the ocean of the east coast. To their left, stood hills that rose from the sea and stretched upwards like immense, green hands to hold the clouds.

That night, after the men had shared two roasted *manicous*, three *zodomeh* and some freshwater crabs called *bacs*, Entahso asked François, 'What was your name before the slavers changed it?'

'Dioub,' François answered, 'I am Wolof. In my village, I was a cattle herder – and the one with the fine fingers that did not shake. People came to me when they had thorns in their skin.' And he continued to speak, calling back memories from great distances . . .

Dioub's village had learned from clanspeople fleeing south that the Fulani cavalry were moving from the north, expanding their grazing land, and raiding Wolof and Oyo villages for captives to barter for European goods. The village elders argued throughout an entire night before deciding to abandon the village. The young herders wanted to remain and fight, until the chief asked how they would defend themselves against mounted attackers with flintlocks. So camels were loaded with materials for shelter, and with bags of grain and dried meat; and the village moved east, deeper into tribal lands among clans that would not be waiting in welcome. An entire morning had passed before Dioub noticed that Iptisam, the daughter of his father's cousin, was not with them; neither was her twin brother, Hamani. In panic, he sought his cousin. 'Lossa, where is Iptisam?' he asked.

'Iptisam's leg has a *kurkunu*,' Lossa answered. She cannot walk, and Hamani has taken her to the cliffs. They will hide there until she can walk again. They will find us. They will wait until the Fulani move on. They will find us.'

'No! Lossa, the Fulani will find your children. Iptisam will become a slave. Hamani will become a slave. Ah! Why did you not tell us?' Dioub shouted.

'And who would carry her?' Lossa responded angrily. 'She will be safe. She would slow us down if she came with us. I did what was best for everybody.' And he turned away, tears streaming down his face. Ahead, his wife was looking back and whispering through the most unutterable of all griefs, 'Iptisam . . . Iptisam . . . .'

Dioub ran to find his father and brothers. 'I am going back for Iptisam,' he said, and hurried off before they could stop him. Two of his brothers moved as if to come with him, but Dioub and his father spoke in unison, 'No.'

He ran most of the way back to the village, hoping that the Fulani were still days away. Hamani, from his lookout among the massive rocks high on the cliff side, saw him enter the village and called out loudly when Dioub was halfway up to the place he was sure they would go to. Hamani's voice carried easily through the desolate quiet, and Dioub answered happily. The Fulani scout sitting under a large acacia tree heard the cries and thought that at least he would have a captive or two to barter.

Hamani took Dioub to the small shelter among the rocks where Iptisam sat, her right leg stretched out so that they could see the skin, shiny and stretched over an ankle so swollen that her foot resembled a brown and purple gourd. On the outer side of the foot was a white blister that the worm had provoked as it sought to break through and release its progeny. Dioub ignored the streaks of red dust and tears, and looked with leaping, contented love at a face as perfectly oval as a hen's egg. He felt his belly spasm in sympathetic pain as she moaned, and wished that he could transfer her suffering to his own leg. 'I will pour water on your foot,' he said to her. 'That will stop the pain and the worm will start coming out. I will start pulling it out, but that may take two or three days. Then we must hurry to meet the village. The Fulani are still many days away.'

He poured some water from his gourd on the blister, and almost immediately it burst, releasing a thin, milky fluid and in the centre of the open wound, a cream-coloured worm protruded, exuding more fluid as it advanced. Dioub broke off a thin branch from a shrub and began scraping the bark away. When the worm had emerged about one finger joint in length, he wrapped it carefully about the stick, and rolled the stick delicately between the forefinger and thumb of each hand until he sensed that the worm was about to break. Then he stopped, waiting for the worm to advance, and repeated the process. The breaking of the blister brought immediate relief to Iptisam, and she rested her head against Dioub's shoulder. 'My parents and the other children . . . are they safe?' she asked.

'Yes. Your mother is suffering. But we will find them,' Dioub answered.

Hamani nodded assuringly, 'It will be easy to find them.'

The next morning, Dioub surveyed the village and its surroundings for an hour before he asked Hamani to go down to the river for water. While Hamani was gone, the couple lay on the ground holding each other closely, hoping that Hamani would not come back too soon. They became alarmed when he not returned long after he had been expected.

Iptisam heard the slight tremor in Dioub's voice as he tried to hide his alarm. 'The boy must be playing in the river . . . I will go and get him.'

'I'm coming with you,' Iptisam said.

'Can you . . .?' Dioub began.

'Yes! I will walk,' she answered.

They walked around the village, calling out her brother's name softly. At the river bank they saw Dioub's gourd and were about to call out again, when three Fulani armed with swords and spears rose from the reeds. 'If you run, we will kill you,' one said. 'Now lie on the ground . . . both of you. Put your hands behind your backs.'

When their hands were secured at the wrists, they were ordered to stand. The Fulani who had spoken reached for Dioub's robe and tore if off, leaving him naked. He walked around the prisoner and spoke to the others, 'That's a good one.' Next, he tore off Iptisam's clothes. 'Um-hm,' he said, then noticed her swollen leg. 'We cannot take the girl . . . she will not be able to walk.'

One of the men took Iptisam by the arm, and dragged her screaming into the bushes. Dioub roared and ran awkwardly after her. The Fulani turned and, almost contemptuously, smashed the pommel of his sword into the side of Dioub's head. When Dioub regained consciousness, it was almost dark. He was lying under a large tree, and his three captors were sitting a short distance away around a small fire, drinking tea and arguing over who would take him to the slave caravan and how they would split his price. Dioub wondered briefly why the men spoke Hausa, which they knew he understood, before he

21

realized they had ceased to consider him as a anything but a commodity to be traded – like a cow or a goat. His chin scraped against the iron collar his captors had placed around his neck. His hands were still secured behind his back, but the rope had been replaced by iron shackles. There was no sign of Hamani, and the men ignored his repeated enquires about Iptisam. He resolved to refuse all food and drink, but they offered him none.

They let him go a little way into the bushes to relieve himself, and on his return, one passed him a cup of water that stank of goatskin. When they rolled out their bed mats, the leader tied a cow-bell to his neck collar. They left him sitting on the ground and lay down to sleep. They did not think it necessary to warn him not to run away.

Dioub was grateful when the sun cleared the hideousness of his first night of captivity. Several times he had tried to kill himself by holding his breath, but had found that impossible. He stopped after the third attempt when someone kicked him and ordered him to be quiet.

The Fulani made breakfast quickly, and gave Dioub another cup of foul water; one pushed a piece of hard bread into his mouth, and his hunger forced him to eat. The men had not mentioned Iptisam or Hamani, and he knew they were both dead: Hamani must have put up a fight. He forced all thoughts of Iptisam out of his mind. The group headed north, walking quickly and stopping only when the sun was high in the sky and the edge of the savannah had begun dancing in the heat. Later that day, they stopped at an abandoned village, and Dioub was allowed to drink his fill of well water. This time, they removed his hand shackles and passed him some salty dried goat's meat and a larger piece of bread.

They continued walking for another day, and late into the evening, until they came upon a large camp of Fulani horsemen. Dioub was left outside a large tent while the men went inside to report their activities. That night, Dioub slept again in the dirt and shared the warmth and fleas of a dog that had sidled up hesitantly and curled up at his back to show its gratitude for not being kicked and cursed. He was roused from sleep before the sun rose, and after a quick meal of mash and roasted goat, he was led away by one of his captors through the camp to the wide road that would lead to the slave caravan.

At noon on the third day, the Fulani pointed to a dark spot on the edge of the savannah and said simply, 'I will leave you there.'

The wind brought them the sound of cries and curses and the smell of excrement from the camp long before they could see the inhabitants. At the gate of the compound, the Fulani was greeted by some men who embraced him and with whom he joked for several minutes before they turned to observe his captive. 'So, Ahmadou, you will want a bride's price for this worthless thing?' one joked, indicating Dioub with his chin.

'You go to bed thinking of ways to cheat your wife of sleep,' Ahmadou replied, to the others' great amusement.

Another man led Dioub away, while Ahmadou remained to haggle over his price.

Over the next week, more slavers came in, leading one captive, and sometimes as many as one hundred slaves. Most of the prisoners were young healthy men; there were few women and children. Many bore tribal scars that Dioub had never seen before, and some men were so tall and thin that he thought they must bend before the wind. Every eye was set on the edge of the plain, refusing to look directly upon any neighbour, or any stick or tent in the camp. Occasionally, they forced their hands upwards to wipe the dust of dirt and powdered dung from inflamed eyes, or they pushed it out of their mouths with swollen tongues because their mouths were too dry to spit. The children moaned softly, having lost their voices days before from incessant crying. The arrival of each group was marked by the barking of camp dogs resentful that even less food would be thrown to them.

When it seemed that the camp could no longer provide sufficient food for all the slaves, the Fulani and their allies began picking out the slaves and lining them up, ensuring that no one was near to another of the same tribe. Other unshackled slaves linked the captives together by short chains fastened to their neck collars. The women and children were shackled separately from the men. Then they set out again, a long black chain of abased, broken and wailing humanity. Ahead, alongside, and behind them rode slavers muffled against the dust, obsidian eyes dulled by the loss of all joy and compassion. They spoke little, except when ordering a slave to hurry or to stay in line; more often they used their whips of plaited leather or the shaft of a spear or a bamboo rod. Occasionally, a captive would stop and fall to the ground, refusing to move even when the drivers rained blows and abuse upon him. The resolution was always the same: the slave would be unshackled, dragged into the bushes and decapitated. Along the route, the places of dispatch were marked by small assemblies of vultures and marabou storks, so glutted that they would ignore the fresh corpses and stand at the sides of the route to stare at the slow procession. The marchers kept their gaze to the ground to avoid stepping on bones or sharp rocks. They no longer cared to brush away the flies crawling into their mouths and eyes, or to hold their breath against the stink of their bodies and of the wayside dead.

They marched west for several days, until the smell of the marshes and the sea reached the caravan. Even the most desolate quickened their pace, as if the ocean would wash away their filth and desolation. And with the greatest irony, it began to rain: blinding white sheets of stinging rain, sent hissing into their faces, washing the grime off their bodies and turning the red dirt of the road into mud. The slaves cupped their hands to collect the first fresh water they had had in weeks, to rinse away the foulness in their mouths before drinking. Some cried silently in gratitude for that small gift.

When the rain stopped, they were able to see through the cleansed air the squat brick fortresses of Ouidah on the Dahomey coast and, riding offshore, great boats with impossibly tall and straight masts. They marvelled, even in their misery, at boats so big that a man could walk from one side to the other of a vessel and not disturb its balance.

The drivers led the captives into large covered enclosures with thick walls of clay bricks, where the men, women and children were separated. The men were chained by their neck collars to ring set into the walls. The women and children had their shackles removed and were put into other rooms secured by iron gates. Here, they were fed more generously with mashed vegetables and dried fish. They learned in whispered fragments of conversation with the caretaker slaves that they were being prepared for long sea voyages to lands in the west, and that only the healthy ones would survive.

The morning after their arrival, they were chained together again and led into a large courtyard, where they were examined and selected by Europeans accompanied by the slave drivers. Some of the children screamed in terror at the sight of the white men, thinking their skin had been peeled off. Most of the slaves chosen for the ships were men. A few women were picked out, but no children. The last would be sold to Fulani and Touareg traders.

Two weeks later, Dioub's group was ordered out of the slave houses and led to the port. They were taken in groups of twenty in lighters to the slave ship, *Fougère*, moored at anchor in deeper water. On board, they were pushed below decks into dark holds that stank so hideously that some of the captives began vomiting, earning themselves threats, curses and kicks from the crew. They walked over grated floors to tiers of wooden bunks where they were signalled to lie, and where each one was pinioned by leg and arm irons so that they could shift slightly but not rise. They were forced to crawl into their places and to lie flat, because the small space between each bunk and the one above it did not permit an occupant to sit up.

Since his captivity, Dioub had fought against panic and resistance, and had largely avoided the notice and whips of the indefatigable guards. He carefully noted everything that went on around him, looking for an opportunity to escape. He knew it would have to be done furtively because he had seen the punishment meted out to those who had attempted and failed: their heads were impaled on stakes on one wall of the prison. But his captivity in the dark, stinking hold was beyond his endurance, and suddenly his fear rushed out like a clawing, unrestrainable feral thing that tore out of this throat, screaming at his captors and at the boards above that appeared to be pressing downwards to crush him. Slaves on the deck began pushing back, refusing to descend willingly into hell; the guards below hesitated, and for a moment seemed ready to bolt out of the holds. But several crew members armed with clubs and belaying pins charged down the steps to the commotion, striking out wildly at everyone in their way until they came to Dioub. They fell upon him and would have beaten him to death if an officer who followed them in had not pushed them away, shouting, '*Assez! Assez!*'

Dioub was caught in a strange dream: the earth was heaving, he could not force his eyes open, and around him were voices calling so softly that he thought for a moment they were leaves rustling. '*M'bibima ... M'bibima ...*' the voices said, over and over. Much later, he would learn that the whispers came from Bariba captives remembering the great land in which their country – and his too – lay; the land that he would hear the Europeans call Africa. Slowly, he began recalling his panic and the beating that followed. He surmised that his eyes must be swollen from the blows; his entire upper body hurt so much that he could only take short shallow breaths. The rocking reminded him of a camel's motion, and for a time he tried to force himself to pretend that he was riding a camel, but the reality of his situation overwhelmed that fantasy, and he had to struggle to constrain another fit of panic. Another sensation spread from his hand, and it comforted him into a shallow sleep. He murmured contentedly, 'Iptisam?'

A voice whispered in Hausa, but with a different accent, 'I am Maimouna.'

'Maimouna? Why are you here?' he asked, puzzled to hear a woman's voice, remembering that the men had been kept separate from the women.

'You are lying near the women,' she answered. 'There are not many prisoners in this part ... perhaps they are expecting you to die. I can hear that you are in pain.'

'Can you see me?' he asked.

'No. It is too dark.'

'Was it your hand touching mine?' he asked.

'Yes,' she answered. 'You called to Iptisam when I touched you. Was she your wife?'

'No. She was not yet my wife. In another year, I would have had enough cattle for the bride price,' he explained, and they both fell silent.

He tried to force open his eyes, and to roll on his side towards her, but the efforts hurt unbearably. He waited until the pain had ebbed, then whispered, 'Maimouna?'

'Yes?' she answered.

'Will you touch my hand again?'

'Yes,' and she brushed his fingers gently.

'My name is Dioub. I will remember you,' he said, and fell into a fitful, painful sleep filled with nightmares of pursuing monsters that attached themselves to his wrists and ankles with claws of iron.

Later in the day, he heard the sound of iron locks being opened and wooden planks being pulled back, then voices shouting in strange languages. Eventually, someone spoke in Wolof.

'It is time for you to eat and relieve yourselves. We will release you, one bed at a time. If you cause any trouble we will throw you into the sea. Make yourselves ready to come up.'

Dioub followed blindly as he was released from his shelf-like bunk and reattached by a neck collar to another slave. At the step, he stumbled and fell back, choking and bringing down the man in front of him. He waited for the whip and the kicks, but the slave behind him helped him quickly to his feet. He quickly murmured thanks in Hausa and in Wolof. His helper did not answer, but kept a hand on Dioub's elbow.

The pull of the neck chains and prodding from the guards' clubs directed them to the stern of the ship, where they perched on swaying benches slippery from the waves and filth, to relieve themselves. They returned to sit on the deck, to eat an indescribable stew made of salted meat and fish and vegetable scraps. Even before they were done, the guards were hauling on their chains to get them back below deck.

The next day, Dioub was able to open his eyes, but only for brief moments because the glare of the sun, directly and off the sea, hurt too much. He wanted desperately to see Maimouna's face, but the women ate and returned below decks before the men went up, so he did not expect to see her while they were at sea. After two days, when he could open his eyes fully again, he would turn to his left and stare into the darkness where Maimouna lay, giving her faces, always-smiling faces; clean hands with long fingers; and a slim, lithe body with wide hips like Iptisam. He would ask her repeatedly to describe a feature and would dwell on it for hours, wanting her to compare the colour of her eyes to a wood, a rock, a pigment or a spice. Hours later, he would ask perhaps about her eyebrows; until, exhausted or bored, she would fall silent. Once, she asked about his face, but he told her he had grown a beard and did not know how he looked now. He sensed that made her smile.

'Did the women in your village think you were handsome?' she continued.

'Yes, I think so. Iptisam was a desirable woman.'

27

'Did you have many suitors?' he asked.

'I had a husband and a daughter,' she answered. 'I was my husband's fourth wife. My parents said he gave a good bride-price for me.'

'That is good,' said Dioub, surprised and annoyed that he was jealous.

In the days that followed, he used recollections of her voice and his images of her face to preserve his sanity. He had considered jumping into the sea after he had seen one muscular captive wrap his arms around two black guards and jump overboard, taking them and three other captives chained to him. The crew members who witnessed the act shrugged, cursed the slaves with greater vehemence and continued their work. The ship did not turn around.

Three weeks out to sea, the ship seemed to hasten westward more quickly as it lightened its cargo of slaves. Dysentery swept through the holds in bloody waves that reached above deck, and would claim one quarter of the crew before the *Fougère* reached port. Sometimes, so many slaves would die at one time, that others would be relieved of their shackles to help throw the stiff, wasted corpses into the sea.

## Chapter 4

# A younger land

Seven weeks after leaving Ouidah, the slaves heard the harsh call of seagulls and saw, when they went up to eat, a land of the most intense green with tall sharp hills of the same deep green. The wind brought them the smell of forests and smoke, but the smells were more delicate than the ones they remembered, as if the new land were younger. The sight of land raised the spirits of the crew and the guards, who would walk among the slaves, saying cheerfully, 'This is your new land . . .' pausing with expressions of surprise when the slaves did not show their gratitude.

The *Fougère* remained anchored offshore because they had arrived too late for unloading the slaves. Early the next morning, the ship docked and the crew and guards hastened to get the slaves off the ship. A long line of chained Africans made its way from the ship to a collection of red brick buildings with barred windows. Inside the compounds, they assembled in the yards, where they washed with water flowing through troughs.

Again, the men were kept separate from the women, and Dioub experienced a suffering greater even than his captivity: he was terrified that he would never see the face of the woman he felt had kept him alive through a voyage of the most unspeakable horror. He vowed then to endure whatever the slave masters and this strange country visited on him until he could see Maimouna. Although he never dwelt on it, afraid that he would voice his intent, he was convinced he would not die in captivity.

For a month, different guards with different faces and accents woke the slaves at sunrise and set them to work, returning generous and immediate punishment for the slightest show of recalcitrance, until most of their victims learned to hide their frowns and hesitations. Even their hatred for their captors, which had kept them awake at night, began to ebb, and was replaced by a tired acceptance that eroded the memories of joys and wishes, and all thoughts of rebellion. Dioub studied his guardians with the same intensity he had studied his cattle for illness and the savannah for signs of predators. They would have been surprised at how much of their language, habits and vanities he understood.

When the auctions came, each walked to the platforms to be prodded and examined with no more than the mild discomfort of a customer being fitted for a suit of clothes. Dioub studied every black woman's face with trembling intensity, hoping that his instinct would identify Maimouna. No woman returned his gaze. Eventually his vision blurred from the tears welling up in his eyes. He was tempted to shout out her name, hoping that she would answer and he would see her before the guards assaulted them, but he did not want her beaten.

At the end of the day, groups of purchased slaves were marched to the port to be taken by small ships to plantations near the coast; other groups set out on foot along dirt roads to inland farms. Dioub's group marched south of the port town, following a gravelled road that led over the hills that ringed the town like a green wall. Near evening, the slaves arrived at a sugarcane plantation that looked from the top of the hills like an endless plain of upright feathers. 'This is the plantation of Principale,' announced an old slave who had come with the French foreman. He looked back at them, smiling with the satisfaction of a confident shareholder.

The day after their arrival, they were assembled in a yard before the great house, where a priest sprinkled them with water, read loudly from a book, and brandished his right hand like a holy cutlass over each one as if to sever their last bonds with humanity. The priest gave the slaves new Christian names. Dioub became François.

For the next year, François became the invisible slave, never complaining or avoiding work, or pleading exhaustion when others fell exhausted in the cane fields from the heat of July and August. The overseers began trusting him with reduced supervision, and even allowed him small second helpings at the quick meal breaks. On Sundays, he was favoured with a piece of cooked meat from the leftovers of the plantation manager's table. If the other slaves were jealous or resentful, François was unaware of it because he spoke little to the other slaves. He did know that some called him '*L'étrange*' – The Strange One. He asked to accompany the hunters on their monthly sporting expeditions, and studiously observed the handling and workings of their firearms. When one noticed his fascination and jokingly asked him if he would like to fire a flintlock, he refused, pleading terror. On these outings, he memorized every path, stream and hill. His French had improved to the point where he understood almost everything overheard or addressed to him. On the rare occasions when he could speak to other slaves from neighbouring plantations, he would ask about a Hausa slave named Maimouna. But beatings and other indignities had taught the slaves discretion and few would admit to knowing anyone with an African name.

On Christmas Eve night, a year and a half after François's arrival at Principale, the slaves were allowed to gather in the yard to watch the festivities prepared for the owner, who was visiting from Europe with his family and friends. After two hours of feasting, the household moved to the great hall, where a small orchestra of old slaves were waiting. As the guards moved to the front of the crowd for better views, François whispered to some men standing in the shadows. And softly, slowly they merged with the darkness beyond. If others saw them leave, they did not say so when the dancing was over and they were ordered back to their huts. The next day every slave was questioned and whipped: none could, or would, give any information about the escape.

*Chapter 5*

# Maroons

François led his band of five men swiftly along one path that he knew well enough to follow in the dark. The others followed panting and stumbling, listening for the soft padding of his feet on the trail. Before leaving the farm, they had stopped at their huts to arm themselves with knives, axes, machetes, and tinder and flint for starting fires. But they had not been able to take any food. François planned to rob small outlying farms for supplies and weapons. The next day, they sat under some trees at the top of a hill overlooking the plantation, and they forgot their privations as they laughed at the search parties setting out towards the coast in the belief that the slaves would avoid the snake-infested hill forests.

Later in the day, the runaways set out for a small farm that lay to the west of Principale. They found it in the evening and spent the entire next day observing the five occupants and studying their movements. They attacked one hour after all lights had been put out, throwing lighted torches on the thatch roof. A few minutes later, as the family rushed out, the runaways felled them with stones, then rushed to slit their throats quickly. The only sounds had been the panicked cries of the farm household.

The raiders found one musket and a small supply of powder and lead balls. They took all the food they could carry and some clothes.

Word of the killings spread as quickly as horse and boat could carry the message. Reports came in of massacres in so many distant places on the island that the maroons were said to have supernatural powers; reliable sources said they were led by a witch doctor whose eyes shone green in the dark, and who could fly through the densest forest without touching a tree.

Children were threatened with stories about the *diablotin* – the evil spirit – of Principale, and the governor of the island was petitioned to send his militia to hunt down the maroons, or to post small contingents of troops at the major plantations. The governor offered a reward of fifty francs for the head of the renegade leader. For months at a time, the maroons seemed to disappear, and when rumours would spread that they had died in the forest from snakes, or from eating poisoned fruit, word would arrive of a nighttime massacre at a farm or plantation. The farm owners began using mastiffs to guard their homes and guards were posted in every building and throughout the slave quarters.

As it became harder to raid the farms, the maroons moved back east to the coast. They moved cautiously along the small beaches, eating sea grapes, and sea urchins and whelks they found among rocks on the shore.

One day they caught the smell of smoke and followed it to within sight of a Carib village. After some discussion, François decided to approach the village and offer the Caribs some of their arms in exchange for food and help with shelter. They walked along a path that ran towards the village, until they were stopped by a small pile of skeletons. All the skulls were crushed as if by axes or clubs. Dioub looked at the fragments of skin and hair. 'These were blacks,' he whispered. 'There must be other maroons. These have been killed by the Caribs. Let us leave this place.'

The maroons returned to the rainforest. From there, they would emerge periodically at night to raid insufficiently protected farms and settlements. Miraculously, they had not lost any of their members, but they suffered severely from insect bites, malnutrition, and skin and lung infections from the damp of the forest.

On their way to reconnoitre a farm one day, they heard the sound of voices and the commotion of travellers not yet accustomed to moving through the forest. They set up an ambush, but found their targets to be a band of exhausted, bleeding slaves. François called out in Hausa, 'Are you runaways? Speak quickly or we will kill you.'

'We are looking for the *Diablotin* of Principale. We have escaped from the plantations of Printemps and Morne Douce. My name is Sivien ... I am Ga,' came the answer in strongly accented French.

'What business do you have with the renegade?' François asked.

'We need safe passage through the forest. We are going to the hills in the west. There are said to be runaways living safely there. Are you the *Diablotin*?'

'Come forward, one at a time,' François ordered.

The pitiful group of six men and a woman did as directed and, after being searched, followed the renegades back to a temporary camp. For most of the night, the newcomers answered innumerable questions about happenings on the plantations, and were asked to repeat, again and again, the rumours and stories surrounding the maroons. The men were pleased with the reports of their supernatural powers. François was especially interested in what the newcomers knew about the hills to the west. He questioned them about the minutest details until they pleaded that they knew no more than they had told. The hills were safe because they were protected by deep gorges that made it impossible for attacking forces to advance in sufficiently large numbers to overcome even minimal defences. There were stories brought back by the slave porters and conscripts who accompanied the army, that cannon were ineffective against defenders because the hills were so steep that the cannon had to be aimed almost straight up and their shot did not travel very far. In fact, rocks rolled down the hillsides killed far more soldiers than the army could tolerate. After two years of pursuit, the colonists found it more effective to use stories of cannibalism by the maroons and massacres by Caribs to reduce the attraction of escape from the plantations.

There was little argument from François's men about heading west. It was clear that their raids were becoming increasingly difficult and soon would not be able to provide enough food and supplies. Their journey west meant even less to eat, and after one week, one of François's men, the woman and two of the men among the newcomers had died of exhaustion.

Despite their miseries, wounds and afflictions, there was never a suggestion of returning to captivity. The hills in the west quickly became an obsession: the subject of every conversation and the expected end of their journey.

A ridge of unscalable cliffs forced the maroons south, and into their encounter with Mabouya and Entahso. Two weeks later, they all stood tired and almost naked, looking at the sea of blue glass and the hills they already considered home.

Suddenly, all pains abated and if François had not stopped them, several of the company would have gone rushing and calling through the forest, seeking other maroons. 'We did not come this far to be killed by our own. We will go slowly . . . follow the streams and look for smoke. In time, they will find us.'

'What if they are Caribs?' someone asked.

'No,' Entahso said. 'Caribs do not live in the forest. They will not live far from the sea.'

It was Mabouya who first saw the plume of smoke on the hillside. It suddenly appeared through the clearing among the trees on the banks of a stream they were following. Immediately they hastened their pace, each fighting to remain calm and to refrain from shouting. They followed a small path through a narrow gorge for some time before they realized that they were on a used trail. As they paused to discuss the discovery, a large rock hit the ground two arm's lengths from François, who was leading, showering them with sharp splinters and mud. Above them, a voice asked in French, 'What do you want here?'

'Maroons,' François answered. 'We are looking for shelter in the hills.'

'Come through slowly,' the voice replied.

The band marched through the gorge and emerged an hour later in a small clearing shaded by massive *balata* trees. Three black men emerged from the shadows, studied them carefully, and looked with surprise at Mabouya. 'Carib?' one asked, pointing to Mabouya.

'Yes,' François answered. 'He has been with us for a long time. He saved out lives in the forest.'

The newcomers looked at each other in wonderment as if they had just been informed of a miracle.

'Why is he carrying an African drum?' the same man asked.

'He is a drum master,' Entahso said quickly. 'I taught him. I am Nzo. I was master drummer of the Pende.'

The three men considered this for a moment and decided that they needed more witnesses to these mysteries. 'Give us all your weapons. All. Now come with us,' the leader ordered, and beckoned them to follow him. Some time later he said, 'My name is Baptiste and this is St. Juste and Innocent,' indicating the others of his trinity.

They walked uphill for four hours before arriving at a small settlement of five houses. There were two old men, six younger men, four women and three children standing near the largest house, and gazing with intense curiosity at the arrivals. 'Maroons,' announced Baptiste, whom they assumed was the village leader. 'Bring some water,' he said to the women.

The villagers had called their hill, '*Mère de nuages*' – Mother of clouds – because clouds seemed to spring from the leeward side of its summit. The name had contracted in time to Manuage. The settlement had existed for three years, and there were even older villages in the hills. These villagers had escaped when a boat taking them to a plantation further north had capsized. There had been more survivors, but the others had died in the forest. They were rescued by slaves who had escaped previously, and taken into the hills. Two years earlier, a company of soldiers had come within a day's march of the hill but had suddenly turned around the left. Since then, they had not seen any more whites.

They helped François and his men clear the brush at one end of the village and showed them how to construct the small huts of poles and thatch they called *ajoupas*.

Mabouya showed the maroons which fruits in the forest were edible and how to trap agoutis. He promised that if they were able to contact other Caribs he would get from them maize, beans and cassava, but he would have to go back to the coast, because the Caribs did not like living in the forest. Baptiste did not show much enthusiasm for that proposal, fearing that Mabouya could return with a war party.

After several weeks, when their wounds had healed, and they had regained most of their health, François became restless. He suggested raiding expeditions on plantations in the north for food and women, arguing that their lives would be healthier if they could plant crops and raise goats and chickens in the hills. And how could the settlement continue without women? Baptiste would consider all these arguments silently and after long thought would say as before, 'Not yet.'

One night François told Mabouya and Entahso that he had decided to search for a slave woman he had known on the ship that had taken them from Africa. Mabouya was ready to set out immediately. Entahso hesitated. 'Who will take care of the drum?' he asked.

'Entahso, you will stay. Mabouya and I will go alone,' François decided.

The next morning, they informed Baptiste, and to their surprise, he asked that they take a youth named Michel. Sivien also asked to come.

Michel guided them swiftly through concealed paths and across rope bridges that spanned the gorges that protected the hill settlements. In three days, they had reached a small plantation. They sat in the woods at the edge of the fields, observing all activities until darkness sent the slaves to their huts. That night, the four feasted on roasted chickens and yams.

During the next six months, François would set out on the darkest nights, when clouds obscured the stars, to steal quietly among the slave quarters, moving from hut to hut calling Maimouna's name out softly. His companions wondered how he could find his way in the dark, and he explained that after careful observation, he could remember every path and obstruction, and would then follow the picture in his mind. The rumour spread among the field slaves that the voice belonged to the spirit of a man who had died of grief after his wife was stolen by slavers, and now the ghost had come from Africa looking for his lost wife.

As they sat looking down at the plantation of Emilion, which occupied a valley just south of Principale, François was contemplating giving up his search: his companions were becoming restless although they had been eating well and had stolen some chickens and vegetables, and a number of tools and machetes. François promised to try two more plantations and then they would simply kidnap some women and return to the hills. That night, he crept among the mud and wattle huts whispering, 'Maimouna,' and almost cried out in surprise when a sleepy voice said, 'Next hut. Who is it?' Then the speaker must have fallen asleep again. At the next hut, he tried three times before his constricted throat allowed him to call her name.

A hoarse, familiar voice replied, 'Dioub,' as if she had been expecting him. He moved quickly to the door and waited in breathless agony as voices inside complained about being stepped on. He felt the heat of her body and caught the scent of her body before he saw her. He found her hand. 'Come,' he said, and hurried her through the fields and into the trees at the edge of the plantation.

The next morning he was already sitting up when the others awoke. His eyes were fixed on her face when she turned towards him. He saw, beyond the film of sleep, two large eyes opening to take in the sky and the forest around them; a small nose with slightly flaring nostrils, and lips set in perpetual questioning. For a long time they looked at each other, recalling whispered words and small touches from long distances and times. They were silent, because they could not find words good enough to say.

Later in the morning, they watched as the plantation owner set out with two other white men armed with guns, and four men, slaves presumably, to look for Maimouna. Then François and his companions crept down to the fields, picked out four women slaves working near the edge of the cane fields and in the cover of the tall reeds. The women suddenly felt hard hands cover their mouths, and strong hands guide them to the forest. Maimouna explained to the women that they were being taken to freedom, and without waiting for their opinions, François led his group quickly through the forest towards the sunset.

On the way back to the hills, Maimouna insisted on walking directly behind François, and not with the other women at the end of the line. She tripped constantly, because she would not take her eyes off him, fearful that he would vanish into the black and green darkness that she found so disturbing. They had not said very much, trying to replace their chosen images of each other with the rough realities of strange faces and shapes. She was apprehensive when night came, wondering whether he would let her touch his hand again. When they lay down for the night on beds of *Heliconia* leaves, he did not take her, as she had expected, but lay close enough to touch her hand. And he fell asleep while she was still brushing his fingers.

They brought back tubers of yams and *eddoes*, three hens, one rooster, and clothes they had taken from the plantations. The village heard several grand versions of exploits that would have exhausted the gods of war. That night, Mabouya took the drum from his hut and wiped it clean of the dirt and dust of long neglect. Later, the villagers felt the ground shake and the wind rush loudly through the village as Mabouya made the drum speak again. In the other settlements among the hills, small groups of black people listened in wonder to the pounding of hooves on dusty, limitless plains, and of great storms pushing against the sky before retreating and throwing themselves to the ground in loud release.

After the celebration, the listeners looked carefully at their surroundings and listened well to familiar voices for assurance that they had not been transported to a new land.

In the days that followed, Sivien acquired a wife; another of the rescued women went to share Innocent's hut. The other women hesitated for a week, then quietly went to help St. Juste and another man repair the thatch walls of their *ajoupas*.

*Chapter 6*

# A thread through time

Since their return, Mabouya had become increasingly melancholic.
He would walk restlessly around the village, then climb the hillside
above the village to sit among the red and purple ground orchids
to stare at the sea for hours on end. One night he said to Entahso,
'I am going to the coast. I must be with my people again.'

'But your people are dead,' Entahso protested.

'There are other Caribs,' Mabouya said simply.

The next morning he was gone. Baptiste wanted to search
the forest, thinking he was lost.

Entahso stopped him. 'He has gone to look for other Caribs,'
he said.

Baptiste was aghast. 'They will kill us,' he cried.

'No. No,' Entahso assured him. 'He just wants to be with his
own again.'

'But the drum . . .' Baptiste wondered.

Entahso shrugged. 'Perhaps he will come back,' he said sadly.
'Mabouya is like a thread from one time to another. The thread
can be broken, but it is a strong thread.'

Mabouya's dejection vanished as soon as he left the village.
In three days he had reached the hills that cradled the bay at
Manatee. He did not go down to the ruins of the village, but sat
under a grove of pandanus palms, listening to the hurrying
wind for the voices of remembered faces. He skirted the village
when he climbed down to the shore, and turned south to
search for other villages.

After several days, he came to the longest beach he had ever
seen. At the far end were yellow cliffs, and at his feet the sand
was littered with fragments of red rock streaked with yellow,
white, purple and black bands. He recognized the place he had
heard the older people of his village call Geroulie, where the

Caribs had landed when they first came to the island. There were no signs of habitation, but he was certain that the Caribs would never abandon this place. He walked to the groves of sea grapes and *Ipomea* vines beyond the sand, sniffing the air for the smell of smoke. Then he headed for the cliffs. Suddenly, he stopped, knowing there were people observing him, feeling their gaze like fine pricks on his skin, hearing their heartbeats and breathing like a multitude of small drums. 'I am Mabouya of the Manatee clan,' he said calmly, as if he was already sitting among them. And he moved to sit on a rock, with his back to the sea, looking down at the ground and waiting.

After several minutes, a voice said, 'All the people of Manatee are dead.'

'I am Mabouya. The chief of clan was Mapipi. The shaman was Kilibri. My father was Carana. My mother was Baroumie. I am the last of the Manatee clan,' he replied.

After another long silence, the voice said, 'Walk towards the cliffs.'

Mabouya rose and turned left. He did not turn around at the sound of footsteps behind him, and shortly he was flanked by two Carib warriors. They looked with interest at his weapons but did not ask for them. As they walked, he told them of his apprenticeship with a black drummer – a story that he would have to repeat innumerable times, because these Caribs had heard of the legend and wanted the entire story. He related his adventures with the maroons, their journeys through the forests and hills, and their raids on the plantations. Each story was greeted with gasps of 'Aaaah,' and sometimes, one would ask for a particular wonder to be described over and over, until the original story was lost. And he told them of his loneliness.

The men took him through a mangrove swamp, warning him to walk along the interlocking branches and not to step on the mud and so leave footprints. Eventually, they came to a rocky ledge between the cliff and the swamp. There, the Caribs had built a small settlement on a dome of volcanic tuff. They had cut steps leading to the top of the ledge and had erected a palisade of posts around five houses built of posts and thatch. In the centre of the settlement was a deep pit with long channels radiating from it. This collected rainwater for drinking. More steps led to a small cave up on the cliff face which they used as a lookout.

41

The chief was sitting on a log in front of the largest house. Around him was the rest of the settlement. Mabouya counted seven men, ten women and five children. 'I am Coubari,' the chief said and waited for Mabouya to tell his stories all over again.

That night he slept in the house of Parai, one of the men who had found him. The next morning he accompanied the men to an adjoining bay with a rocky shore, where they collected shellfish and caught small red snappers. Mabouya was careful to stay out of the surf, remembering that the sea still hunted for him. He learned that he was the first Carib of another clan they had seen in a year. Several times, white soldiers had come by boat to the bay, and had scouted along the shore, but the clan had always escaped detection. Coubari had considered making peace if the colonists came too, but the rest of the clan had objected, declaring their intention to fight any invaders who settled near the bay.

It was several days before Mabouya thought of Entahso. He missed his old tutor, but had come to the belief that each had now arrived at his own destiny. So he set his mind to forgetting the black people of the plantations and the hills. Sometimes at night he thought he could hear the drum, but when he went outside to listen, he would hear only the roar of the wind and the chirps of crickets.

One evening, a loud wailing rose up from a neighbouring house. Outside the house, the villagers were gathering to look at the bodies of two children lying on a mat of woven grass. Their faces were swollen and their skins were covered with red weals and pustules. The next day, the other three children had died of the same illness. Two days later, a newly married young woman and her much older husband died. An unspeakable terror gripped the village as these people, who did not fear individual death, contemplated the extinction of the last of their race. Mabouya remembered seeing that illness before. He had seen the rough eruptions of the skins of some children at Manuage. He had brought this contagion to Geroulie.

He was not surprised when Coubari sent for him. 'You have brought death to Geroulie. If you remain here any longer, we must kill you. Leave now.'

The Caribs looked away while he collected his belongings. As he walked away, Parai began tearing his house down to burn.

For three years, Mabouya wandered through the scrub forests along the southern coast. Only once did he meet Caribs again – for the last time. He was collecting whelks from rocks at the base of a small cliff, when two old people walked around a bend in the shore. He heard their gasps of surprise, and his hand reached for his machete before he turned and saw them. For several seconds they stared at each other, their eyes filled with immeasurable sadness. Then the old woman offered him two whelks. He shook his head, showing her his own. The two old naked Caribs nodded, and walked on without saying a word. Some distance away, they looked back at Mabouya, his gaze still fixed on them; then they disappeared around another bend.

Occasionally, he came upon small fishing settlements of destitute blacks, in areas where the soil was too poor to grow anything but manioc. In two of the villages, he noticed that some of the children were almost as light-skinned as whites.

One morning, he awoke to the sound of thunder coming from the sea, and watched in trembling awe at opposing lines of great ships sailing past each other, blowing down each other's masts with roaring blasts of smoke and fire.

At other times, he walked through old battlefields strewn with blue and red fragments of clothing, and the broken weapons of young men who had come on the orders of gout-destined old men to claim the lands of others by the facile expedient of planting flags on poles. He saw the spirits of men clutching viscera spilled by sabre cuts, and others looking without understanding at the tableaux painted by their brains and blood on the trampled grass. All around him were the cries of frightened boys asking for escape from this strange land, begging for mothers and sweethearts. He ran quickly from these places, away from the shadows, into the cleansing brightness of the sun.

He awoke suddenly one night, certain that he had heard the sound of the great drum. He crawled out of his small *ajoupa*, and he could hear very clearly in the still air the song of the dead. As soon as it was light he set out for the forest and then towards the west.

No one challenged him as he climbed the road to Manuage. The village had grown larger and was filled with strange faces. Children ran from him screaming, and a couple of small dogs settled down to barking themselves hoarse with delight at this unexpected event. Most of the adults were away in the gardens along the hillside, but some were already returning to the disturbance. François and Entahso tried to outrun each other in their haste to get to Mabouya first. Entahso was too filled with emotion to speak, so he held on to Mabouya's hand and cried. Mabouya looked at his grey hair and wrinkled face with surprise, recalling the other Entahso of his memory.

'The thread did not break,' François said mysteriously to Entahso. The other nodded happily.

François was now the headman of the village they now called Tambour – after the drum. Maimouna had borne him first a daughter, and then, to his immense relief, a son. The daughter was named Violette, but those who lived nearby called her 'Violente' because of her temper. The boy was gentle and introspective. They named him Hamani.

It was a full day before Mabouya could ask about the sound of the drum that he had heard some days ago. 'I thought you were dead,' Entahso explained. 'It was hard for me ... I do not have too many years left. Not enough to teach another *Maître du Tambour*. I am glad you have come back, Mabouya.'

Mabouya nodded. Soon he would have to start forgetting: Manatee, Geroulie, and the old couple gathering whelks. He was now, even among these friends, inconsolably alone. He almost regretted that Entahso was still alive. Otherwise he would have swum out to sea, and let the water swallow him – as Mapipi had warned.

New runaways arriving at Manuage told of battles between the French and the English for possession of the island. The changes in governance had made little difference to their lives except for the irritation of having to take orders in different languages every other year – or so it seemed. Eventually, the French ceded the island to the British. The new overlords immediately took offence at the occupation of their land by runaway blacks, and sent frigates to bombard settlements along the coast within reach of their cannons. Inevitably, they came to Manuage, and sent an emissary accompanied by a black interpreter to order the maroons to hand over their weapons and descend the hill in single file so that they could be registered and sent back to their rightful owners.

François listened in silent amusement, then offered the interpreter asylum – which he accepted – and relieved the tired official of his onerous sword, and sent him back down the hill with a gourd of fresh water.

Six months later, an expedition of soldiers, accoutred in heavy red woollen coats and assemblies of leather belts, marched on Tambour from landings to the south of the hills. François sent messengers to the settlements and villages on the lower slopes of the Manuage and to the small bays to the north, warning them of the soldiers' approach and offering them the shelter of Tambour. Those who had hesitated abandoned their homes when refugees arrived to tell how their villages had been burned, the inhabitants beaten or killed, and their gardens razed.

François appeared rejuvenated by the threat. He led teams through the forest, preparing ambushes with rocks and pointed stakes; he set Mabouya to preparing quantities of poison for arrows and spears, and they prepared covered pits along the main paths to Manuage.

The soldiers made no sudden attack on Tambour. For two weeks they methodically surveyed the area, dismantling traps, and clearing wider roads to the hills. Then they dragged mortars to the base of the hill and laid siege to the nearby villages of Latainer and Mahôt, demolishing them within minutes. Before the smoke cleared in the villages, the soldiers rushed in, slashing with bayonets and sabres at anything that moved; then they burned anything left standing. Their progress stopped at the pass where Baptiste had once challenged François. The English commander sent captives ahead of his troops, to be killed by traps and rockfalls. Then they moved swiftly, only to be met by a shower of poison arrows and a wall of machetes wielded by berserk defenders driven by images of slave drivers, whips, chains and branding irons. Rivulets of blood coursed down the road from Manuage, until the combatants were separated by a wall of slippery, bloody corpses.

A trumpet sounded, and the soldiers began retreating. The defenders looked around in horror at the carnage and consoled themselves with the hope that the battle was over. A second trumpet sounded, and a fresh group of soldiers rushed forward, their muskets belching lethal smoke and fire. And through the smoke came glinting slivers of bayonets and sabres. The maroons fell back in despair, but were determined to die with their women and children. François threw himself again and again at the enemy, miraculously evading their blows, lunges and pistol shots. His entire body glistened with his own and the blood of others.

Entahso searched fearfully for Mabouya, and when he found the bloodied Carib – his face fixed in a wild grimace that looked like joy – he pulled at him. 'The drum!' he shouted, 'The song of war. Go! Please go.'

Mabouya hesitated, then saw the desperate demand in Entahso's tired voice. 'Goodbye, my father,' he called out to Entahso and ran up the path to Tambour.

The soldiers felt the ground shake as if some subterranean giant were shaking itself awake. The trees began to shiver and the sky turned the colour of bloody ash. The air grew hot around the soldiers and filled their lungs with the stink of war: of burning bodies and decaying flesh, of severed limbs and spilled bowels. Their mouths filled with the metallic salt of blood, and green bile poured from their mouths, even between their clenched teeth.

The redcoated men turned about and made their way silently down the mountainside, their eyes glazed with fright and despair.

François and his remaining defenders did not pursue the retreating soldiers. They moved closer together, trembling from the sound and vision of war and destruction. No one moved until the drum fell silent. Then they pulled the torn and pierced bodies of their dead from the carnage, and carried them wearily up the hill to the clustered wretchedness and tears of their women and children. They found Entahso's body with his skull split open. In his clenched left fist was a length of thread stained red with *annatto*. The villagers buried the bodies at the bottom of the hill, near the field of battle; they lay Entahso's body a little higher than the others, his hand still clutching the stained thread.

Mabouya brought the drum to the burial ground. He sat on a rock near his friend's grave and played the death song. For three days and nights he beat the drum, but so inaudibly that the sound did not leave the graves. On the morning of the fourth day, the the villagers saw him lying on the ground, curled up with his knees drawn almost to his chin. Even François lacked the courage to see whether he was alive. Mabouya rose when the sun had cleared the mists from the hillside, and he walked slowly to his hut. He refused help from those who offered to carry his drum. That evening, he rubbed his entire body with ashes, rinsed himself clean with spring water; then, when his body had dried, he covered himself with *annatto*. Afterwards, he ate four small bowls of food that his neighbours had brought and laid at his door.

The soldiers never came back.

Five years later, the slave ships stopped coming to the island; and abandoned crewmen fought for work on the plantations they had formerly stocked. In England, the voice from the frail body of William Wilberforce had proved more difficult to ignore than the imprecations and implorations of distant rum-producers. The abolitionist fervour of his evangelism failed to yield to measured exchanges, and left their Lordships so harried and shaken that, one month after his death, they sent dispatches to the Indies informing stupefield governors that the slaves had become subjects of the British Crown.

The freed slaves abandoned the plantations. Some moved away to settle the river valleys that ringed the island and open-ed out to the sea. Others moved to the hills, to the villages of Citronelle, Latanier, Mahôt and Amande. Only a few moved further up the hill. The men and women who continued to Tambour were the last to be transported from Africa. The god *Ogun* came with them, as did his festivals of *Macumba* and *Kélé*.

More runaways came in small canoes and rafts from the French colonies, bringing with them an African-French creole that would become the language of the island. Their numbers did not diminish until the members of the National Assembly in Paris found their elegant discourses on Voltaire and Rousseau befouled by the stench of slavery – and the provocations of a M. Victor Schoelcher. So the rulers of the republic enjoined the governors of the colonies to precipitate themselves upon their slaves with the sincerest cries of '*liberté, égalité,* and *fraternité*', and make them Frenchmen and Frenchwomen.

## Chapter 7

# Maimouna

The people of the villages that clung to the flanks of Manuage were amused at first by the faint hints of rotten eggs in the air, joking that a neighbour had hoarded eggs for too long. But the smell grew stronger throughout the day, until it stung the eyes and left children crying and gasping. Near sunset, the ground shuddered, and the hill rocked like a canoe hit broadside by a wave. The dogs and chickens ran yelping and screaming into the forest, and people fell to the ground in panic, calling to long neglected gods and spirits. A few moments later, the hill seemed to rise, then settle sharply as the world roared with an explosion that deafened everyone, and while they were still prostrate with fear, the sky darkened suddenly and black clouds fell on them as a hot grey ash. The noise came again and again, until their hearing died and they felt each roar as a blow to the chest.

Those bold enough to look up saw flashes of crimson lightning in the southern sky, but there had been no sign of rain and none fell. For hours, the noise, tremors and ash fall continued. François gathered Maimouna and their children and crawled with them into the forest, believing that the huts would soon burst into flame. At times, the hill would shake violently like a dog ridding itself of the dirt it had lately been rolling in. Maimouna sat beneath a tree, clutching Violette and Hamani, now limp and silent with terror. François looked fixedly at her as if searching in her eyes for an answer that was not in his own mind. She leaned towards him as if to explain, and as he came closer, she pressed her face tightly against his – for the first time. He nodded his understanding: they did not expect to see each other again.

The fall of ashes stopped during the night and the clearing air brought the sight of a new spectre: a river of red fire poured into a valley to their west, kindling the forest trees even before it touched them. They watched it advance arrogantly like a flat red snake with scales of yellow flames, watched as it engulfed a river, which exploded into a white billowing curtain of steam that rushed high up into the darkness as the water continued to push against the wall of liquid fire.

Another faint tremor, and the noise stopped, as if that fulmination had exhausted the earth; and a colder wind sighed its relief down the hillside.

No one slept that night, except for two old people and a newborn child killed by the fumes or ashes. Morning showed to the living, hills and valleys white with ash except for the black rope of still-smoking rock that the lava flow had become. They tried sweeping away the ash, but only raised clouds of choking grit that the wind would return to cleaned spaces. The rain came one day later, and turned the ash into chalky mud that ran down the hill in grey rivulets to cloud and clog the streams and rivers; but the springs near Tambour continued to flow with clean cool water.

News about the recent cataclysm came swiftly from hill people anxious to tell of their own personal witness to the eruption that had blown away the entire top and part of the side of a small volcano. They related how hot stones had set fire to the thatch roofs of abandoned huts and ignited even the greenest trees, and how liquid fire had poured from the cleft side like water from broken gourd.

Mabouya said his grandfather had told of the time their people had left another island to the south when a similar event had occured. After two days of darkness – the grandfather said – the clans had put everything they could into their canoes, even into the narrow war canoes, and had come to this island. One year later, some warriors had returned to visit and found the land with new hills and bays. They were unable to find signs of life except for some insects. They fled the island that night, unwilling to sleep in the quiet of death. Mabouya looked around at his listeners, and smiled grimly. 'Maybe the volcano god is hungry again … and is looking for fresh victims,' he said half in jest, but no one smiled back.

Maimouna's nightmares began two nights after the family returned to their hut. Even while the lava flow was still red-hot, the tall thin man coming towards her strode along it as easily as

49

if it were a forest path. At first she thought it was François, and she ran to him to ask why he would do such a foolish thing. But the face that looked back was that of a pig: an abomination so foul that her people would not use the name even as an insult. Yet, to her disgust, she was attracted to the stranger, wanting him more strongly than she had wanted her first husband or François. She followed him helplessly, walking along the hot lava, resisting the pleas of naked women crouching in the bushes nearby, who warned her to turn back before her shame condemned her to live forever in the forest, unable to face her family and neighbours again. But when she tried to turn back, the face that implored her to stay was transformed to one of impossible beauty, shining with the power and dignity of an Ile-Ife bronze, and she hurried to keep pace with him, afraid to lose the promise of immeasurable love.

She followed him to his house of black polished hardwood, and hurried without bidding to his bed. He turned her gently on her stomach and lowered himself on her back. Her anticipation turned to unspeakable horror as hoofed legs pinioned her arms, and a long snout covered in coarse black hairs pressed against her face, while a barbed flaming spear tore its way between her legs and into her belly. She cried out so strongly that she lost her voice immediately. She tried to claw at him, but his pounding held her immobile. After many hours, when she lay limp from exhaustion and pain, begging him to kill her, he rose and chased her out with harsh grunting laughter. She did not hide in the forest as the other victims had warned her, but forced herself back to the village, determined never to reveal what had happened, and to find some way of exacting vengeance. But two months later, she rose quickly from bed one morning to vomit, and she knew she was pregnant with the monster's baby.

Her screams woke François and the children. She threw herself off the straw bed and rolled on the floor of the hut, tearing at her belly. Two neighbours called from outside, and François answered that Maimouna was having a nightmare, before he bent to quiet her. By then, she was sitting on the floor, looking around in bewilderment until the comfort of awakening, and François's voice calmed her.

The nightmare recurred twice more, exactly as the first time, with the monster laughing mockingly that she could never leave him.

And as if in confirmation, her monthly blood flow did not come. The next month, with the hard certainty of misfortune, she began to vomit on awakening, and her breasts became uncomfortably tender. Her terror was impossible to hide; and when his anger, cajoling, threats and reassurances proved futile, François sent frantic messages to the other villages asking for the help of someone who could chase an evil spirit from his wife.

One morning, a thin figure climbed the road to Tambour. The villagers marvelled that so wasted a man could carry himself and the large leather pouch that swung from his shoulder. 'My name is Ayo. I am looking for François,' he said to the small group that had gathered in curiosity. Then he sat on the ground, apparently to relieve his legs from the combined weight of his massive head and eyes that bulged from the accumulation of knowledge from two continents.

When François arrived, Ayo said to him, 'I am a Yoruba priest. My name is Ayo. You wanted to talk to me?'

François nodded, and Ayo followed him back to his hut. On the way there, François tried to tell the Yoruba priest of his wife's incomprehensible fear, but Ayo silenced him. 'The spirits will tell me everything.'

He asked that he be left alone with Maimouna in the hut, and most of the village assembled dutifully but determinedly at the doorway of the hut. Inside, Ayo took the stool that Maimouna placed before him, and told her to sit on the ground and face him. Slowly and delicately, he placed his hand into the pouch and picked out polished black stones, bones from a small animal, cowrie shells, and placed these on a square of red cotton cloth spread out at his feet. He made a circle of the stones, another with the shells, then tossed the bones in the black ring and repeated this in the circle of white shells. He stared silently at the scattered bones for so long that Maimouna looked up, wondering whether he had fallen asleep, but she looked down again quickly, away from the two pits of darkness in Ayo's head. He reached again into his bag and withdrew a small glass vial. 'Water,' he said to her, and when she came back with a cup, he poured some yellow powder into the cup and stirred it with a finger. He handed her the cup. 'Drink,' he ordered.

Maimouna raised the cup and was startled that the liquid was tasteless, but spread an immediate warmth through her body that brought an uncontrollable urge to sleep. She fought to stay awake, but her body slumped forward, and she found herself floating near the roof of the hut, looking down at her body and the priest. She heard him ask questions, and heard her body answer, telling him about the nightmares, the man with the pig's face, and her horror of the thing growing inside her. As she spoke, Ayo rocked backwards and forwards, making a low monotonous humming sound.

At the end of the story, Ayo replaced his stones, shells and bones, and smoothed the dirt floor where they had been. He called François into the hut. 'Your wife is haunted by an evil from a place she lived before she came to Manuage. The baby is yours but she will not believe that. I cannot tell you what to do, but she will try and kill the child. She is sleeping. Put her on the palliasse. She will wake tomorrow.'

He accepted a chicken and two large yams for his fee, and left for his home, his frail body further burdened by a hen that would have dragged him into the forest if her legs had not been trussed.

François did as Ayo had said, and found himself in the centre of great debate, speculation and advice. He took Mabouya by the arm and asked him to walk further up the hill with him, towards the springs that fed the village streams. 'Maimouna is possessed by a spirit from the plantation of Emilion. That is what the Yoruba said. I do not know what to do,' he said.

Mabouya nodded and said nothing for a while. 'Do you want me to speak with her spirit?' he asked finally.

'Her spirit?' François asked in surprise.

'Not the one that possesses her. Her own spirit. It will tell me things she cannot say with her mouth ... things she has forgotten,' Mabouya replied.

'How can you do that?' François asked uncertainly.

'She can smoke with me. The smoke calls the silent voices back.'

François nodded. He did not understand what the Carib meant, but he was afraid of the strange thing that possessed his wife.

'Bring Maimouna to my hut tonight. Come when the others are asleep ... and the dogs are quiet.'

Deep in the night, François and Maimouna went quietly to Mabouya's hut. Inside, the darkness was relieved only by a red glow that brightened and dulled behind a mist of acrid smoke, as Mabouya sucked on a pipe. In the faint light, they edged closer to Mabouya, and sat on the floor to face him. The Carib began humming softly as if calming a baby, and soon his guests were forced to struggle against the overwhelming comfort of approaching sleep. 'No,' Mabouya warned.

So they let the sleep come. François immediately fell into a vortex that carried him down forever towards its ever-receding termination. He let his mind scream, as no sound would come from his mouth. Maimouna felt her senses sharpen so acutely, that she found herself listening with amusement to the sound of moths flying past the hut and to the footfalls of ground insects as they scratched through forests of grass. Again, she was floating above the hut, calling to Mabouya to follow her down the hill from Tambour, over the forests and rivers, swiftly across deep valleys and gorges, to the sharp demarcations of the northern plantations. They went directly to the once-prosperous plantation of Emilion; the sharp edges of its abandoned fields and buildings already softened by the returning forest. Maimouna pointed to a main wing of the great house. She refused to go nearer, and Mabouya entered alone through an open window with shutters that flapped in the wind like a beckoning. In the room furnished with discarded, once-ornate furniture, a man lay snoring on a bed with three remaining posts. Mabouya's gaze was immediately drawn to his face, with its nose so strongly upturned that it resembled an animal's snout. His skin had a yellowish tint, like the pyrites that Carib children collected from seaside cliffs.

The captain's family had contributed unhesitatingly towards the purchase of the plantation, so that they could be spared further shame by the son whose campaigns into the beds of maids and country girls had been more fruitful than his efforts against the English.

The misgivings that he had carried to the Indies – condemned to exile with a consumptive wife whose thinness discouraged any affection – fled at his first encounter with the strong-bodied black women who kept their gaze to the ground. That had appealed to him. And when he stole into their huts at night, and was close enough to see into their faces, the darkness and his tightly closed eyes again shielded him from the expressions of hatred and contempt.

His wife had discovered, without surprise, the light-skinned babies accompanying their mothers to the fields and playing in the yard of the great house. One of these she selected, because of his riveting ugliness, to be raised in the house and to eat with them, despite the captain's protests. The child's looks served to diminish the captain's appetite for food only. So he tolerated his wife's small whims out of respect for her beckoning death.

With inexplicable irony, the captain named the boy Beau. And for years afterwards, strangers would recoil in startled discomfiture when he was presented. Like his father, he found his conquests permitted only by the forced submissiveness of slave women. He was particularly fascinated by the woman who refused to accept the name Josette given by the priest, and who was still called Maimouna by the slaves. His certainty that she would not yield willingly so fascinated him, that for weeks he lost his appetite for nighttime invasions. Eventually, his craving sent him to her hut, but his courage failed when the light of the small oil-lamp he carried reflected a coldness in her face that drove him away in angry humiliation. The next night he was back, propelled by a courage briefly loaned by a bottle of brandy. He chased away the other women who shared the hut, and immediately threw her upon a straw mattress and tore her clothes from her. He then kicked off his shoes and pulled down his pants. But the brandy that had emboldened his will had neutered his flesh. In his frustration and rage, he rammed her with a still-virile hand, bloodying them both. Once again, her impassive face, and the eyes that would not leave his, drove him stumbling and crying from the hut.

He avoided her presence after this, and it was only the cost of replacing a healthy slave that saved her life.

Mabouya went to the sleeping man and squatted on his chest. The sleeper's eyes fluttered open and he stared in absolute terror at the apparition before him. He struggled to wake from the nightmare, but his feet would not move. Nor could he lift his hands off the bed to throw off the weight that was slowly suffocating him. He tried to gasp but whenever he exhaled, he was unable to expand his chest again. His heart fought desperately against the remorseless pressure, fluttered, then stopped.

The Carib left through the window and said to Maimouna standing outside, 'We can go now. Your baby is safe.'

Their journey back was so swift that Maimouna saw the terrain below as a hurrying blur. In the hut, the three bodies sat very still, their eyes open but not seeing. After a few moments, Mabouya moved to open the door to let the smoke out. He shook them by the shoulder. 'Go,' he said.

As they hurried back, Maimouna wanted François to hold her very closely, to warm her against the coldness that did not come from their nearness to the clouds. Tomorrow, she would make herself sing old, half-remembered songs of childhood.

Their baby was unhesitatingly called the most beautiful boy anyone had ever seen. People from other villages came with the firm purpose of seeing the baby that others said was so handsome that men and women cried with joy at seeing it. Soon reports went about that the child was responsible for strange, happy events at Manuage: enemies were reconciled, harvests were better, and animals were giving birth to double litters. Most wonderful of all, the boy's beauty grew as he matured, and women's faces burned in embarrassment as they allowed immodest thoughts about the child to penetrate their minds.

His parents named the boy Nicholas. So everyone called him Sonson. He grew tall and spare, like his father, but his beauty surpassed that of any ancestor François or Maimouna could remember. He spent most of his adolescence evading the young women of the hills and neighbouring villages, who abandoned restraint and propriety in attempts to capture the enchanting but quick-stepping Sonson. Unaccountably, the person he admired most was the semi-reclusive Mabouya, who had not offered close friendship to anyone else since Entahso's death. But Sonson would sit for hours with the old Carib while he made small clay figures – Carib gods, he told the boy – or he would accompany him to the forest to search for *annatto* and medicinal herbs. But despite his relentless pleading, Mabouya would not teach him the songs of the drum. 'You cannot hold the drum,' Mabouya said cryptically one day.

'I am strong enough to hold it ... and my arms are long enough to hold it. How can you say I cannot hold it?'

'The drum is for a master who does not want to hold anything else. You, Sonson, will want to touch many more things. You will not have time to care for it.' After a pause, he said sadly, 'And you are not a mabouya.'

'No, I am not a Carib. But this is an African drum,' Sonson argued.

Mabouya broke into a rare smile. 'Yes,' he said, 'that is why Entahso continues to beat it.'

Sonson shook his head in annoyance at Mabouya's enigmatic comments. 'And who will beat the drum when you are dead? Umm? You will not let anybody else touch it. Ah! I cannot understand you. Nobody can understand you.'

Mabouya looked at him regretfully for a while, then said, 'Sonson, I will help you make your own drum ... and I will teach you how to make it sing. But my drum is not for you. One day, I must pass it on to another person. But not you. That is all I have to say.'

Sonson's frown lessened slightly. 'A real drum?' he asked, trying to mask his excitement.

Mabouya nodded and stood up, stretched, and started up the hill to the pasture of pink mimosas to wait for his people's canoes to come again across the sea. Sonson stayed back, and later in the evening, celebrated the excitement of his anticipation with an eager young woman in an abandoned *ajoupa* at the edge of the forest – near Entahso's burial place.

## Chapter 8

# The chronicler

The villagers celebrated the end of the dry season with the ceremony of Kélé. This required the sacrifice of a male animal, and they selected an unmated white ram whose coat was unblemished by any hint of another colour. François sent word to the other villages at Manuage, and a gift of sweet potatoes to Ayo, the Yoruba priest. Ayo arrived massively encumbered with a bag – even larger than his head – containing sacred objects that included meteorites, Yoruba and Ibo statuettes of black iron, and Carib and Arawak axe heads. He refused all help with his load, although at times his legs faced defeat by the incline. He assured everyone that he was in the best of health, when he at long last – and to everyone's relief – made his way to a stool at François's doorway. 'We will have a visitor today . . . for the Kélé,' he announced. And as they waited expectantly for further information, he astonished them with his next words. 'It is a white priest. He is interested in these things . . . Yes . . . Yes. I gave him permission to come. He will not interfere with our business. And he is a good man . . . I know him. Um-hm.'

The people of the hills did not receive this news with visible enthusiasm. But no one stepped forward to quarrel with Ayo. Some brave ones muttered words about senility and presumption, but did so quietly.

As Ayo prepared the site for the Kélé ritual, Maimouna took François aside. 'When the priest comes, I want him to baptize the children,' she said.

François stared open-mouthed at her. 'What are you saying? You want some crazy man to throw water on the children and call them names? They already have names,' he almost shouted.

'No, it is not that. This is a strange country . . . It is not our country. Maybe there are other gods here. I do not know. But if there are, I want the children to know about them.'

'I do not know who put these things in your head, and I do not know whether the people of Tambour will want that. What do you want me to say? That we must become Europeans? After what they have done to us?'

'But what if our gods are not here? They did not protect us from the slavers.'

François took too long to think of a good answer to this, and Maimouna walked away with a look of quiet determination that he did not like.

Later, if he found the opportunity, he would ask Ayo about this. And strangle the little man if he laughed at him. He frowned in irritation, annoyed that Maimouna had rendered tasteless his previous ruminations about eating the sacrificial ram.

Ayo cleared a circular area with a straw broom, and in the centre made a small altar of the sacred objects he had brought. He walked around it several times, rearranging items, then finally nodded his satisfaction. 'Good. Let us start,' he said.

But Mabouya did not come alone with his great drum: Sonson followed him, carrying another drum – tall and shining black, like its bearer and his father. François's chest almost exploded with pride; Maimouna smiled to hide her greater apprehension, uncertain about Sonson's proximity to a strange man and strange powers.

Just then, the crowd turned towards the road that led into the village. Some children were pointing excitedly down the hill, and the smaller ones were running screaming and calling excitedly as they ran towards the adults. 'Must be the white priest,' Ayo said.

Soon, a grey-haired, sunburned man, dressed in a coat and trousers that were once white but were now stained brown by the soil and forest, and sitting astride a dejected and exhausted donkey, rode into sight waving enthusiastically and calling out greetings in French, English, Yoruba, and KiSwahili. The stunned crowd made way for him; and on sighting Ayo, he slid off the immediately relieved donkey, and went to take the Yoruba's hand, which he shook with a vigour that threatened to detach Ayo's limb.

'This is the Abbé Joubert,' the bruised and shaken Ayo said.

The Abbé nodded happily to the world around him, took his mount to the edge of the clearing where he tethered it, and returned to sit on the ground near the cleared circle. The children assembled in massed ranks to stare unblinkingly at the beaked nose, as scarlet as a cock's comb, and grey eyes that seemed to be two large suspended drops of water. Ayo returned to the ceremony.

The drumming began. The black priest led the chants in Yoruba, with the gathering answering the words he had taught them but whose meanings he was already beginning to forget. The celebrants found it difficult to continue singing, wanting to listen to the drums calling to and answering each other, filling the hillside with wide, heavy sounds that flew upwards, around them, echoed from neighbouring hills and cliffs, then plunged headlong into unforgiving chasms far below. Children clutched tightly at their parents' hands and clothes, their young senses still able to feel the summoned intangible presences that swirled and danced among them.

After two hours, when some of the dancers fell to the ground in exhaustion, Ayo signalled for the tethered ram to be led to the centre of the circle. Two men took hold of its hind legs, and François held on to its rope, so that the ram stood on its forelegs with its neck stretched over the small altar. A woman dressed in white handed a finely honed machete to Ayo. He poured a small quantity of liquid from a small gourd on the blade, and began a rhythmic chant, his eyes fixed on the neck of the animal. Slowly, he raised the machete, and with a speed that seemed impossible in one so frail, the machete flashed downwards, severing the ram's neck so quickly that its head lay on the ground before blood spurted in two scarlet streams onto the altar. For a surprisingly long moment, the ram remained standing on its forelegs as if uncertain about what to do next, then its legs buckled and it collapsed near the altar. Ayo skinned and quartered the animal, handing one hindquarter to François, saving another for himself, and sharing the remainder with those who had helped with the ceremony.

The villagers dispersed slowly, afraid to miss any wonders that might follow the white priest. When he eventually managed to disentangle himself from the thicket of small fingers and legs, he sought out Mabouya. 'M'sieu Mabouya, it has taken me many years to find you.'

'Why were you searching for me?' Mabouya replied.

'Our church keeps the stories of everything that happens on the island. I found many incredible legends about the Carib who has a magic drum that remembers the songs of Africa. Now, M'sieu Mabouya, do you not think such a strange thing would be of the greatest interest?'

'Well, I cannot deny that I am a Carib. But how did you find me?' Mabouya asked.

'I asked,' Abbé Joubert answered simply. 'Eventually I found Ayo, and we became friends. After many years, he trusted me enough. He told me how to get to Tambour.'

Mabouya nodded, 'Um-hm.'

'My interest is in the legends of colonized people. It will be a great loss to the world if important knowledge is not preserved.'

'Why do you not get a wife and plant crops? Like a useful man? Instead of chasing stories?' Mabouya asked.

'Ah! For the same reason that you keep the drum. Even though it is not yours. It is something I have to do. Sometimes, when I am tired, I think of doing something else. Then the emptiness of living without a great obligation opens in front of me and I become like you: to do what I can do better than anyone else.'

Mabouya looked closely at the priest and began laughing helplessly. He fell to the ground clutching his belly, and roaring with laughter as he had done many years before when Entahso told him of animals that weighed more than all the men of Manatee put together.

'At last, I have met a truly mad man ... like me,' he said, wiping the tears from his eyes.

So Mabouya told Joubert about Entahso; how he had wandered into the Carib village of the Manatee clan ... and used the drum to save his life; how he, Mabouya had been apprenticed to Entahso to learn the drum; and about the events and years that had led him to Tambour. 'But I have not been able to find an apprentice. No one wants to send a child to live with an old Carib,' he said. 'Perhaps they think I will eat him,' and he laughed again.

'But I saw a young man ... an extraordinarily handsome young man ... beating a drum with you. I thought he was your apprentice,' the Abbé said.

'That was Sonson ... François's son. He pursues me every day, wanting to be the master drummer of Tambour when I die ... but he spends too much time chasing women and being chased by women. He cannot give his life to the drum.'

'But you are getting old ... who will carry on after you?'

'Entahso,' Mabouya said before he could stop himself.

Joubert looked at Mabouya with the question unspoken. Mabouya looked back puzzled, wondering what could have made him say such a stupid thing.

## Chapter 9

# A different god

The Frenchman slept in the Carib's hut that night. The next morning, Maimouna was waiting with two bowls of stew for their breakfast. All the village children came to stand in solemn attendance to watch them eat.

As soon as they had finished, Maimouna spoke quickly to Abbé Joubert. 'M'sieu Abbé, I want you to baptize my children.'

The priest was taken aback. 'Baptize them? But you do not believe in our God.'

'Since we have to live with your God, then we will have to accept some different things,' she replied.

The priest withheld whatever he intended to say: the look on Maimouna's face advised prudence.

'Bring the children,' he said resignedly.

Maimouna left and soon returned with her adult daughter and sons. The priest faced them with open-mouthed amazement. They stared back in resentful discomfort: Violette almost suffocated with the effort to suppress the many words she could have used for that moment; and Hamani was irritated with trying to explain to his own accompanying family what he himself did not understand. Sonson had argued briefly with Maimouna – but how does one stop the wind blowing?

So Hamani was christened Raphael; Violette and Nicholas kept their names. The children of Raphael and Violette were also christened, but because these were never written and would not be used, they would soon be forgotten. The other parents, not to be outdone, pushed their offspring forward to be doused with water, addressed in Latin, and given the names of French saints. Despite the giggling, they enjoyed themselves thoroughly.

For the rest of the day, the priest made enquiries about the village and its inhabitants: how they had adopted new customs and foods, and what they remembered of their original tribes, songs and ceremonies. The priest used up several quills – made from chicken feathers – writing long notes and making finely detailed representations of the village and its people – to the delight of all.

He left early on the morning of the third day with promises to return. For the next eleven years, Abbé Joubert returned every four months to Tambour. When he stopped coming, the villagers concluded sadly that he had died. They knew of no one to ask about him, Ayo having died two years previously.

When François discovered that his body, in agreement with time, no longer wanted to climb the slopes of Manuage to the upland gardens and pastures, he satisfied himself with sorties to Mabouya's hut, where they would spend long evenings exaggerating past adventures and victories. Every year or two, François would peer ever closer at Mabouya and ask, 'But friend, you do not seem to be getting older. Look at you . . . somebody would say that you were just forty years . . . or even thirty five. Tell me, *compère*, is it some Carib tea you are drinking? Does it help with the women?'

And they would roar with more laughter than the joke merited.

Or François would point out some manifestation of Mabouya's apparently eternal youth. 'Look at me. Only one tooth left, and you . . . .'

'Nine,' Mabouya would interrupt.

'Eh?'

'Last week, you had nine teeth.'

'Well even if I have nine teeth, you have not lost one single tooth. Not one! Open your mouth. Let me see,' François would insist. Eventually Mabouya would surrender the privacy of his mouth, allowing François to count and exclaim triumphantly, 'Ha! Thirty-two teeth!'

One evening, François did not interrogate Mabouya about his miraculous preservation, and the two sat staring for over an hour at the far sea without speaking. Mabouya knew that his old friend would not visit again.

The next day, Mabouya walked to François's house. 'You knew I would not come today,' François said.

Mabouya nodded.

'Last night, I had this strange dream: I was standing on a large plain covered with grass and short bushes, and a woman came up to me leading a herd of cattle. Big, fat cattle with shiny hides. Her face was shaped ... like an egg. A beautiful face that I am sure I have seen before. She kept asking me where I had been; and said that she had tended the cattle in my absence. She was giving them back. And she was glad I had returned. It was a nice dream.'

'Maybe it was somebody you have forgotten,' Mabouya said encouragingly.

'Yes ... Yes. Perhaps. But it was a nice dream,' François said wistfully.

Maimouna was awakened, just before dawn, by the sudden quiet when his breathing stopped. She woke Sonson and sent him to get Raphael and Violette. There was a soft call at her door and the light from her oil-lamp showed Mabouya waiting outside. 'My friend is gone?' he asked.

'Yes,' Maimouna answered.

The next day, the villagers buried François near Entahso's grave. It took her two sons and two other men to carry the wailing Maimouna from the graveside to her hut. She did not leave the hut for two days.

In a small bay, seven miles south of Manuage, a tiny settlement of fishermen and their families had grown into the small town of Rocher. It served as a port for shipment to the north of dried fish, and fruits and vegetables that thrived on the fertile volcanic ash that covered the hills. Once Maimouna had learned that Rocher was also the site of a small Catholic church, she insisted on walking for four hours to Rocher – when the weather permitted – to attend Mass. Soon she was joined by another woman, and within a year, the initial amusement of the men faded to irritation when they were left alone on Sunday mornings to prepare their own breakfasts. The old men followed, not wanting to miss the opportunity to become acquainted with another afterlife. Almost imperceptibly, Tambour, like the other villages of Manuage accepted the church because of its arcane rituals, and the opportunity it gave for wearing clean clothes, seeing old friends and exchanging gossip. The young men quickly discovered that it was also the best arena for competing with their friends for the disinterested but repeated glances of young women from other villages.

The resident priest railed constantly about the savage rituals still practised in the hills, and the villagers would nod sympathetically and return to incorporate some of the church rituals into the *kélé* and *macumba* ceremonies. They did not wish to take sides in disputes between divine powers.

The colonial government arrived in Tambour like a bird of prey on a distracted victim. This time, the authorities sent only one white official, and three black aides armed with rifles, but no ammunition. They arrived on horseback, in mid-afternoon when most of the villagers would be home from church or their gardens. The children were greatly pleased with the appearance of the white official. He was as pale as mist, dressed all in black, with a great prow of a nose, spectacles that magnified his grey eyes, and so tall and thin, that he resembled a starved vulture impatient for the horse beneath him to die. With immediate concordance, the villagers named him *Le Corbeau* – the Crow.

One of the aides announced that Mr. Timothy Bideford was the administrator of the district of Rocher, which included all of the villages on Manuage, and its administrative centre, the town of Rocher. The villagers and the official smiled at each other: the villagers with barely concealed amusement at the official's appearance; and the official face twitched to reassure them that his administration would remain benign as long as they knew their place. Mr. Bideford advised his audience to select a representative to speak for the residents of Tambour, and he turned to leave before anyone could offer him a drink of coconut-water or fruit. But they were still smiling brightly as the officials left. One of the Englishman's aides was shaking with suppressed laughter; the others were frowning mightily.

Maimouna immediately set to work to ensure that Raphael would become the village representative. If she had remembered to ask her chosen candidate, Raphael would have told her he had no interest in village politics that were not related to his crops and small herd of goats. The villagers to whom she casually mentioned her son's many admirable qualities nodded agreeably, and went home to complain about her unceasing interference in their lives.

Sivien stopped at her hut to discuss his arthritis and grandchildren. After he had described the innumerable undeserved afflictions that daily threatened his life, he asked about her. 'Ay! Maimouna. So how is life treating you?'

'You know how it is,' she answered. 'Every day is a struggle. But God will provide.'

Sivien nodded at the words that he himself would have chosen. 'Life will never be as good without François. But we must try and go on,' he mused. 'So how are the children managing?' he continued, obliging Maimouna to bring up the subject of Raphael's reluctant candidacy.

Maimouna responded immediately. 'Tell me if you do not think that Raphael should talk for us with the government,' she challenged Sivien.

'Maybe he would be the best person. But he is not talking for himself. Maybe Raphael is not interested,' Sivien answered.

Maimouna looked directly at him. 'Sivien, tell me what is in your mind. You came to tell me something.'

'Maimouna,' Sivien answered, 'we have become old people together. We saw you as the mother of Tambour. Let the children go now. Let us grow old quietly.'

They sat through a long silence until Maimouna spoke. 'Who do you think would be a good representative?' she asked.

'Baptiste has a good son,' Sivien answered. 'He is a serious man. And his father was one of the first people in Tambour. Yes, Primus will be a good man to talk with the whites.' He paused to reconsider what he had just said, and satisfied, he nodded, 'Um-hm.'

Maimouna turned her interest in her children's futures to her second priority: that of finding a suitable wife for Sonson. She was determined that the chosen would bring more than the convenience of a warm body on cold nights. She set off early one morning, armed with the company of her sharp-tempered daughter Violette, to visit the recently widowed Christophe and his daughter, Ti-Ange. Christophe owned a large piece of land that occupied most of a small valley in Mahôt. Centuries of accumulated volcanic ash, and alluvium deposited by small streams from the montane forests, had created soil that was devoid of rocks and so fertile that Christopher's solitary efforts were enough to keep his family modestly comfortable.

Maimouna had seen Sonson's interest in Ti-Ange growing even faster than the girl's breasts, and she was not about to lose a valuable dowry because of her son's inevitable boredom with another easy conquest.

Ti-Ange was alone in the hut, peeling vegetables for cooking, when Maimouna and Violette arrived. 'Ma Maimouna, Violette,' she greeted them. 'You came to see my father? He is in the garden. I will go and call him.'

'No! No,' Maimouna protested, 'I will go and talk to him. Which way is he?'

Ti-Ange pointed the way and Maimouna set off. Violette scowled for a few moments at her host; then without a word began helping with the meal.

'M'sieu Christophe!' Maimouna called when she could hear the sound of his machete.

The chopping ceased, and Christophe's head appeared above a hedge of vines. 'Ah! Ma Maimouna. But how are you? You look well,' he greeted her.

'God is good,' Maimouna reminded him, then launched into a quick but detailed summary of her latest ailments.

Christophe nodded sympathetically, then gave an even more agonizing account of his travails. 'But what brings you so far?' he asked finally.

Maimouna assumed an expression of greatest solemnity. 'We are growing old,' she said at last, 'and our children will have to manage without us . . . in a little while.'

Christophe nodded gravely.

'You know my son? The second one? Sonson? Well he is interested in your daughter Ti-Ange. And I think Ti-Ange is interested in him – I have seen them looking at each other after Mass. Now Ti-Ange is a very nice girl and it would kill me if anything bad happened between them. You understand?' she asked.

Christophe nodded despite his total befuddlement, but he decided to await future clarification.

Maimouna continued, 'I want to tell Ti-Ange to show that she is not interested in Sonson.'

'But wait,' Christophe protested, 'my daughter is not good enough for your son?'

'M'sieu Christophe,' Maimouna said patiently, 'that is not what I said. What I am saying is that I want Sonson to respect your daughter. If he is interested in her, it must be because he is serious, and will not treat her like somebody he can just drag into some old *ajoupa*.'

'Ah!' Christophe nodded, grinning in admiration of the plan, and unwittingly approving of his daughter's marriage without her knowledge or opinion, and without his prior consideration.

Back at his house, the parents warned Ti-Ange in the most ominous terms that she was not to permit Sonson any liberties of sight, speech of touch with her person.

Ti-Ange, who already had an interest in Sonson that was best suited for contemplation outside the church, was heartbroken. But she promised to observe the sanctions.

Sonson immediately sensed her new coolness the first time he saw her again. Subsequent encounters confirmed his suspicions that she was not interested in him. His pride bruised, Sonson first resented, then became obsessed with the pleasant-looking girl who was not especially beautiful, but whose skin shone like oiled mahogany. His interest in other women languished until only great effort and sweating enthusiasm would prompt sufficient response.

One Sunday after Mass, he followed Christophe and his daughter to Mahôt where, in tearful earnestness and desperation, he pledged to devote his entire life and fidelity to Ti-Ange. Christophe promised to consider, and the next day went to Tambour to visit Maimouna and discuss her son's marriage to his daughter.

The sons of Sonson and Ti-Ange would take the name Christophe and their descendants would farm the valley for many generations.

After Sonson left to go to live with Ti-Ange at Mahôt, Maimouna often went to sit with Mabouya on the step of his front door and talk about the better memories. She remained wide eyed and generous, and her face was beautiful when she died.

Mabouya watched his friends and neighbours wrinkle and bend closer to the earth, listening for death's footsteps. Much of the hillside had been turned into gardens of yams, potatoes, plantains, beans, *taro* and *topi-tambour*. Fierce, stringy chickens roamed freely through the village, leaving little puddles of defiance on territories claimed by undernourished mongrels.

Above the village, goats and sheep diligently destroyed the original forest, leaving a pasture of short wiry grass and pink thorny mimosas, whose leaves closed demurely when touched. Large boulders of hardened lava lay scattered in these small fields, and in the months when the evenings were longer, Mabouya would sit on one of the larger rocks that provided a wide view of the sea, seeing in his memory, large grey canoes pushed by short sharp oars and sails of rough cotton. He would join in the rowing songs of the red-painted men, boasting of conquest and the taking of Arawak women: 'Hai! Hai!'

His place was assured: François had ensured that everyone knew that they all owed their existence to Mabouya. They also feared him because of the many myths and stories surrounding the drum. He was not allowed to garden or asked to help with difficult work. And his small table was never empty. Sometimes, a child would stop at his hut carrying a shirt or trousers, and wondering if these just-found articles would fit M'sieu Mabouya – his parents wanted to know.

The funerals came at shorter and shorter intervals. Soon, he began forgetting names and faces of later generations. Sometimes he would go to deserted beaches on the eastern coast with his drum, sheltering in a small *ajoupa*, and living off wild fruits and shellfish. When he returned, a new set of faces would greet him; then these would grow old. The years came to him too, exchanging the black of his hair for ever-deepening wrinkles in his skin. But it was not until the fourth generation of Tambour's existence that the hill people called him an old man.

*Part Two*

# Chapter 10

# Zacharias

Edouard Christophe had been faithful to his lover, Ti-Marie Charlotte, for the last thirty-seven years of his life. Her gap-toothed smile and quick, generous dimples had lured him to the bushes near her home, beneath her father's coffee and cocoa trees, where he overwhelmed her with an eloquence that astonished both of them, and left her breathless. Her soft body, and readiness to please him rewarded her with the pain and pleasure of five sons, her own home, and his unwavering constancy. They had named their first four sons after the New Testament gospellers, as a small insurance that the saints would be more sympathetic than the parish priest had been over issues of adultery and illegitimacy. The four brothers, like their father, were short and solid, piled with muscle, and seemed to have sprung fully moulded from the brown earth they loved and tilled. The last son came after Edouard and Charlotte had come to see each other as sources of comfort rather than intimacy, and so they were surprised when Charlotte became pregnant, eight years after the birth of John. Charlotte did not share Edouard's pleasure at his virility. They named the boy Zacharias, as if in declaration of finality, and he was immediately called Zaky; just as Matthew became Maffew, and Mark became Mack. Luke kept the simplicity of his given name, but John became Johnny-boy.

Zaky was an uncommonly beautiful baby. Even the dour and tired midwife said so spontaneously. Everyone else in Mahôt agreed and predicted that Zaky would grow up to break the heart of every woman in the parish – which he did. Little girls loved the teenager who grew to six feet at fifteen, with wide forever-laughing eyes, eyebrows dark and smooth as the wings of an oriole, and a mouth that stayed slightly open as if about to kiss another girl. Grown women who should have known better found ways to let him know when their husbands would be in the city; and when they expected to be alone harvesting *dachine* from the dark, hidden marshes that fed the hillside streams. Zaky threw himself into life with an exhuberance and generosity that disarmed jealous men and muted the envy of the boys. On Sunday mornings, long before the sunrise, the people of Mahôt or Latanier or Amande would wake at the sound of Zaky's teasing laughter provoking giggles from a girl, and women would turn to their husbands or lovers and pull them close.

But sometimes, those close to Zaky saw a hot restlessness in him, as if his soul fought to tear its way out of his flesh. At these times, his eyes darted about looking for some lost object, and the women grew uneasy and found other things to do.

Zaky was five years old when his mother and brothers took him to a Macumba festival at Tambour. There, he looked at Mabouya for the first time. The Carib stared so hard at him that he shivered with fright and refused to let go of his mother's hand for the rest of the afternoon. Mabouya was unable to take his eyes off the little boy. He continued to look distracted as if surprised to see the face of someone who had left long ago, and should not have come back.

That night, Zaky screamed himself awake from a nightmare. His screams awoke the others, but they told him it was only a bad dream; and he should just go back to sleep. So he fell asleep fighting the urge to use the chamber pot in the darkness under the bed, and shortly afterwards, wet himself, his bed and bedmate, John.

In his dream, his father had brought him a beautiful drum from Latanier; but when he reached for it, his father turned into the man he had seen in Mahôt with the eyes like black glass. He fought to take his drum back, but the man lifted it above his head and walked away. Despite his screaming, no one came to help him. The house and village were silent and deserted.

The dream recurred for years afterwards, even after Zaky no longer showed any outward fear of Mabouya. But his apprehension of the drummer never waned, and as he grew older, the resentment turned into an obsession to reclaim the drum that he felt should have been his.

Edouard's legal wife, Ma Christophe of Latanier, died appropriately on a Saturday morning, ensuring that her funeral would be on Sunday afternoon, when most of the parish would be able to assemble to recall examples of her generosity and saintliness; and to forget her bad temper and dislike of children. She was aged ninety-five years and two months on the day of her death, childless and alone in a small house even older than herself. Her husband Edouard had died seventeen years earlier, and had willed his eighty-five acres of bananas and coconuts to the five sons he fathered with Ti-Marie Charlotte in Mahôt. Ma Christophe did not die destitute: after her husband's death, his sons – ignoring her scowls, complaints and threats – continued to provide for her needs. One Christmas, they bought her a transistor radio with so many buttons that she was forced to listen to thirty-six hours of carols before a neighbour rescued everyone's sanity by showing her how to turn it off.

People came from as far away as Citronelle, where the paths are lined with the herb that smells more of limes than the fruits themselves, to attend Ma Christophe's wake. They came dressed in white and black, carrying their shoes in their hands because they had to walk along narrow dirt paths, and through shallow streams. In Mahôt, they washed their feet at the communal water tap before putting their shoes back on. Then they assembled in the yard around the house of mourning to announce Ma Christophe's arrival to the heavenly authorities. Her nearest neighbours had the honour of wailing the loudest and declaiming the near impossibility of life without her love and guidance. Her husband's sons had the duty of providing everyone with rum and coffee for the wake that would last two days.

Throughout the evening and until sunrise on Sunday, the body lay in beflowered and perfumed state while mourners filed solemnly through the house. The children grumbled that they were not allowed sufficient time to examine her face, with eyelids pressed shut by two large copper coins, nostrils plugged with cotton balls and mouth secured against gaping by a white ribbon tied over her head. Ma Christophe was securely packaged for heavenly transport.

No one mentioned the absence of Mabouya, the drummer from Tambour, because they knew when he would come. The Caribs had used the word 'mabouya' to mean an evil thing; it

75

was also the name given to the small black gecko that crawled out of crevices at night and was said to attach itself to the skin of anyone who touched it, until someone killed it with the application of a red-hot iron. Some said Mabouya was the last of his people; that was why his skin was copper, his hair was straight, and his eyes were black slits that looked past one's face into all the years of one's life. Mabouya was the master drummer of Tambour, and so, the supreme drummer of the island. His age was a matter of quiet dispute: the oldest villages swore that he was old when they were children; and the ancient parish priest could find no record of the drummer's birth – and he had searched carefully.

The villages did not see Mabouya come into the yard; they were first aware of him as he set his drum carefully against the trunk of an old avocado tree in the yard. He said nothing to anyone as he walked with his head bowed into Ma Christophe's house. The villagers he walked past said, 'Goodnight, M'sieu Mabouya,' although they would have been surprised at an acknowledgement.

At the bedside, he looked at the sunken pallid face and nodded. He lifted his gaze across the bed to the wall, and as if speaking to another presence said, 'She was one of us.' Then he patted the cold stiff hand gently and walked out, remembering the dead woman's ancestor, Violette. So long ago ... but the memory was good to have again, even for a brief time.

The story telling began at ten o'clock. They would take turns recalling the stories that had come to the island with canoes and sailing ships – old stories that were told to speed the spirit on its way, and to give more comfort than the light of their kerosene lamps.

The oldest neighbour spoke first. 'Cric-crac,' he said, using the ritual of beginning that was older than remembrance. 'Cric-crac,' the villagers answered in unison, as they had done for all stories told before. 'There was a time . . . .' the old man continued.

At ten minutes before midnight, Mabouya moved to sit on a small stool someone had put near his drum. He took the drum between his knees and began murmuring to it; then he tapped it gently with his fingertips until the villagers heard its voice: a long, low 'Mmmmmmm,' the sound of unrelievable solitude that belonged to a darkness deeper and more resolute than the one beyond the light of their lamps. 'Um-hm,' Mabouya answered, and his hands began to beat faster. In a moment, the drum would take him to the other place with the people he had known for more than two hundred years.

On the night of Ma Christophe's death, Mabouya sang the Death Song that the African drummer had called from the drum the day he wandered into Mabouya's village. The mourners from the hill villages heard familiar sounds, but did not understand the words, even though it was once their language.

The first murmurings of the drum quieted the crowd; then, as its beat entered the low forest around them, the *tôlines*, tiny tree frogs that pealed like a chorus of church bells, fell silent. Then the most persistent of the night callers, the six-inch forest crickets, camouflaged like tree bark, and invisible even during the day except for their large eyes of exquisite turquoise, stopped their quick 'Craaak . . . crak-crak-crak.'

People huddled closer together; even lovers who had drifted casually into the shadows moved away from the dark. The drum called out and was answered by wind sounds from the high trees, although the leaves hung motionless. The cries were soft at first, like infants awakening and beginning to call for their mothers' breasts; then the drum thundered, and the cries turned to screams, and to the echoing calling-calling of people lost in dark caverns who were answered by the echoes of their own voices. They heard the pleas of people running through the forest, their cries muted by the thunder of Mabouya's drum. Voices came closer, but no one came out of the forest. Even when the drummer's hands paused, the sounds continued, echoing from the trees and rocks and hillsides.

One man, fighting to restrain his discomfort, pumped furiously at the dimming Coleman lamp hanging from a branch behind Mabouya. The bright light from his back further obscured Mabouya's face, and threw the shadows of the mourners into the forest, climbing the trees or plunging into dark spaces. From the corners of their eyes, the villagers saw the shadows dance, leaping to touch the tree branches, spinning, twisting, flinging themselves into the trees and onto the ground with a wantonness and violence that could only have come from weightless and unhurtable things. But when the mourners turned to look directly at the shadows, nothing moved. Often, a person would rub an arm or a neck, to warm away the touch of cold things that had crawled out of caverns and hollows, and out of the night.

They all began to pray, hesitantly at first, then with loud urgency, their voices pushing against the song and thunder from the drummer.

But gently, like a polite host signalling his reluctant guests to leave, Mabouya's drumming slowed, and the blur above the drums became his hands again. Zaky, the last son of Edouard Christophe, stared at the hands and tugged at his oldest brother's sleeve. 'Maffew! Maffew! Look at his hands!'

'Eh?' Matthew asked, looking at Mabouya's hands and seeing only movement.

'Look at the hands!' Zaki urged desperately, 'Look at the colour! What colour do you see?'

'But they're black of course,' Matthew replied.

'What colour is Mabouya?' Zaki asked, his heart thundering.

Matthew hesitated, frowned and said softly, 'He's brown.' The drummer's hands blurred for a second, then with a final thump, the movement and sound stopped.

The brothers moved closer to look at Mabouya's hands as they lay flat on the grimed drum head. The hands were brown, blotched and wrinkled, like the old man's face.

The mourners sat in the yard – few felt obliged to enter Ma Christophe's house in the dark – to await the light of Sunday morning. Mabouya stood and put the drum under his left arm. 'I think I'll carry myself up the hill, now. What time's the funeral?'

'One o'clock,' someone answered.

'Uh-huh,' Mabouya said as he left.

Zaky sought out his other brothers, Mark, Luke and John, to tell them what he had seen of Mabouya's hands. They looked to Matthew for confirmation.

'Truly, I cannot say for sure, but one time the hands looked black and the other time they were brown ... perhaps it was the light. And it was so dark anyway, I don't know ...'

Zaky persisted, 'I was looking hard. And it wasn't only the colour. When the hands were black, the fingers were different ... they were longer. Something else was beating that drum.'

'Shit!' Luke exclaimed 'Look, I'm scared enough tonight. You two go and take your nonsense somewhere else.'

Mark and John were staring silently at the path Mabouya had taken, wondering how on old man could carry that heavy drum up into the hills, and without a light. Mark turned to Zaky. 'And you wanted him to teach you the drum ... the man's a *gens engagé*,' he said.

'Well, even better,' said Zaky with more courage than he felt.

At school, Zaky's teachers loved him too much to push him to excel, and he did well enough to pass the entrance exams to the college in the city. But Zaky refused to leave Mahôt. At nineteen he wanted no more school education; he told his mother and brothers that he wanted to become a drummer and dancer. Charlotte laughed and his brothers teased. But the boy was adamant. So they told him to do what he liked, expecting him to forget his fantasy after a few months.

Zaky worked with his brothers on the family estate. On weekends, he practised with a small dance group in Latanier, which had been founded by a retired schoolteacher from the city who wanted to preserve the old dances. Several times he walked to Tambour to ask Mabouya to teach him the drum. Each time, Mabouya refused, pointing to his two students. 'I can only teach one at a time ... and I have two.'

After another refusal to an especially determined plea, he said to Zaky, 'Someday, it will be necessary to have a new *Maître du Tambour* ... but he must start at ten years old. No one will give me a child to teach. And you are too old.'

'Well, just let me watch you all,' Zaky begged.

'Look, I don't have a clock ... or even a watch. The boys live here. We practise when we feel we have to. No, Edouard's son ... I can't do it. Go to school,' he said impatiently, and turned his gaze to something too far away for Zaky to see.

'I'll ask you again, you know,' Zaky said as he turned away.

'I know,' Mabouya answered ruefully.

## Chapter 11

# The keeper of old things

In April, the cooler winds coming from the Atlantic picked up less moisture, and the days were usually dry and bright. So the people of Rocher were not perturbed by the thick clouds on the morning of their parish festival. By eight o'clock, the sun had hurried the clouds away and the sky had taken on the brilliant intense blue of places where too-steep hills and mountains kept away things that were compelled to make smoke and dust.

Everyone spoke too loudly, hiding their residual tiredness – because the excitement of anticipation and ironing of new clothes had kept them up late into the previous night. All around was a clamour – of shouting at giggling children to be quiet, of fussing husbands and wives that someone would never be ready on time, of worrying that something indispensable would never be found. One should never anticipate enjoyment on such a day: better to be prepared for disaster so that pleasures could be better savoured. Inside, one heard the 'scritch-scritch' of fingers soothing the irritations of collar tags and the other projections of new bodices and shirts; while outside, skirts and pants bought only the day before answered with their own 'swish-swish.' What good would such a festival be if everything went perfectly, leaving the fortunate to agonize about the vengeful calamity that must inevitably follow?

The villagers of Latanier, Mahôt, Laurier, Citronelle, Tambour and Amande crowded into small vans and brightly coloured buses, with names like 'Good Mood' and 'Forever Lovely', to be ferried at dangerous and unnecessarily high speeds to the town of Rocher. Even the drummer Mabouya rode the bus. The driver refused to take his fare, despite Mabouya's insistence – a ritual older than the driver ... older even than his father. The driver also insisted that Mabouya sit at the front with him, but Mabouya's drum was too large to fit, so some passengers gladly gave up an entire row further back, as they had done the year before. This was the only time Mabouya chose to ride in a vehicle, and although he enjoyed the conveyance occasionally, he thought cars and buses were too dangerous to be used as substitutes for walking. He sat smiling despite great efforts to look fierce, pressing against the drum on the seat beside him to keep it secure.

At Rocher, disembarking passengers stood quietly for a few seconds to recover from the oppression of perfumes, hair pomades, sweat, claustrophobia, and travel-twisted stomachs. Then they walked with stiff dignity to the town square to hurl themselves into greeting friends and relations. Their carriages hurried back, guided by tiring drivers reviving themselves with bottles of near-frozen beer. The older drivers took quick shots of whiskey or strong white rum that squeezed their eyes shut, and left them gasping in relish: 'Aaaah!' 'Yes!'

The smell of roasting, frying food guided all to the square, a field on the southern edge of the town. On other days it served as a playing field, and at night as a trysting place for those without cars. And before elections, it served as the pulpit from which failed businessmen and idle lawyers shouted their extravagant plans for the enrichment of all, and, more energetically still, detailed the sexual imprudences of their opponents. Despite the greasy smoke of braziers and stoves, the parish festival brought a greater cleanliness to the square; and all gossip was brought for exchange or favour.

At one end of the field, the Ministry of Agriculture had set up a block of pens to showcase the accomplishments of proud livestock farmers. Most of the enclosures held overfed, freshly washed pigs and sheep, gazing back mildly and languidly at their admirers. The greatest excitement was activated by a brahma bull that, scorning all pleasure in the blue ribbon that hung on the gate of his enclosure, was trying to gouge and butt his way out – encouraged by the screams of the children.

Nearby were the stalls of the vegetable exhibits, where fruits and vegetables of sizes and colours never seen in the markets were touched, rubbed, smelled, and offered to onlookers to judge their weight. Modest farmers – standing at the ready in camphor-impregnated, clean clothes – refused to accept any praise for their bounty, protesting that it was the fruit of heavy applications of well-ripened cow manure, plentiful rain and God's grace. Audiences agreed solemnly, and wondered how the farmers had secured the last benefaction.

For those interested in the latest in scientific developments, the festival organizers had provided a booth manned by an enthusiastic, perspiring agricultural adviser who was demonstrating the use of a Geiger counter for detecting radioactivity. His hands moved quickly as he poked various members of his audience with the detector, pausing often to adjust glasses whose heavy lenses ensured they were constantly absconding down his wet nose. After he had assured his subjects that they were not sources of dangerous emissions, he admitted that there were no radioactive minerals on the island. 'In fact,' he said grandly, 'the only radioactive thing here is the luminous paint on my watch. See?' And he lifted his left wrist to provide testimony; then, by way of punctuating his lecture, he violently prodded his slipping glasses back up his nose.

Having ensured the attention of his audience with this gesture, he brought the counter with dramatic slowness to the watch on his wrist, whereupon the machine began clicking loudly. The spectators held their breath in awe, profoundly relieved that they all wore digital watches.

The music started about noon. Assemblies of massive loudspeakers, painted in sombre black, in contrast to the their cheerful music, flattened nearby eardrums with thousands of watts of reggae and *zouk* tunes. The music should have started earlier, but the sound technician had left after an argument with his girlfriend, who had chosen the site of the festival to discover her unhappiness with his height of five feet. After surveying the field, and taking into consideration her eight-inch advantage, she confided loudly to him that he was 'shorter than a good time.' He confessed his own sentiments about her appetite and greed, and left in his car, abandoning her and the equipment to his curses. The disc jockey eventually found another technician to take care of the electronics. The forsaken lady was left to agonize over choosing among three anxious rescuers.

At five o'clock, the crowd began moving towards an elevated wooden stage with a backdrop of palm fronds. The master of ceremonies showed a group of six musicians to their seats near the foliage, and moved to a microphone to announce the main event of the festival: an 'exposition', as he called it, of folk dances. The members of the band were all old men; and except for Mabouya's drum, their instruments had been passed on from their fathers or teachers. The men moved, seemingly out of habit, to make room for Mabouya in the centre of the group. The band members began their elaborate routine of tuning their instruments, peering intently as if seeing them for the first time, frowning mysteriously, wiping off invisible dust and playing loud discordant notes. Mabouya sat in serene aloneness, occasionally caressing his drum, and looking through slitted eyes at the crowd, searching for an old friend: the archaeologist-historian-painter, hoping they would be able to talk again. Then he saw Zaky and his dance troupe approaching. He grimaced, convinced that the boy would dance to impress him, then ask about playing the drum. Again.

The dancers moved importantly through the crowd, Zaky ploughing through female hearts with his wide, only-for-you grin. The women dancers wore long white dresses, brightly coloured neck scarves, abundant makeup, and they carried perfumed lace handkerchiefs. The men wore black suits, white shirts, and ties of unrestrained resplendence and width. All except Zaky wore black shoes of ancient styles. The six men and five women were old enough to be Zaky's parents or grandparents; it had taken them years to learn the old dance steps, and their own children were too impatient to devote a lifetime of evenings to learning the quick, intricate movements.

The master of ceremonies had many memorable things to say about the preservation of customs and traditions, but surrendered to the shouts of, 'Hurry up! OK! Go home! Let the people dance!' and, most painfully, 'Shut up!' He nodded to the band, and left the stage smiling bravely.

The men and women dancers formed into two lines opposite each other. The men, with hands clasped behind their backs, bowed gallantly to their partners; the women curtsied gracefully; and Mabouya tapped his drum softly to signal the start of the quadrille. The two violins took voice, and the flute, guitar, and shak-shak generously gave themselves up to sound.

Right feet moved forward, left quickly followed, just touching the stage before right feet moved quickly to the right. Left feet tapped loudly, bodies whirled, skirts and jackets lifted. The knock of the dancers heels blended so precisely with the beat of the drum's command, that it seemed the dancers were led by the drummer's hands rather than by long practice.

A proud, comforting silence fell upon the crowd. This at last was theirs, not borrowed or new, to be savoured only occasionally, so they would not tire of it. Some older spectators tried to suppress tears brought on by good remembrances and regrets for irrecoverable time. The young people admitted to envy at the dancers' skills, and made resolutions – that would not endure beyond the festival grounds – to learn the old dances.

The band members played with their eyes closed, as if to assure the jealous music of their abandonment of other, lesser sounds and sights. All except Mabouya. And just before it became dark enough for the electric lights to come on, he saw the bald head and the thick glasses moving slowly through the crowd.

The spectators moved aside to let the old man through, their irritation at his gentle push turning to polite greetings when they recognized him. His head bobbed constantly as if in thanks. As he neared the stage, whispers preceded him, clearing a path, and making room at the foot of the stage. Someone rose and offered him a place on a small bench. He smiled his thanks and sat down. The newcomer and Mabouya acknowledged each other with almost imperceptible, satisfied nods. The drummer leaned back, and closed his eyes.

The dancers stopped after two quadrilles, two *lacomêtes*, a waltz, a mazurka and a *zouk*. They waited until the long applause had completely stopped before descending the stage. The women protested that they could have done better; the men challenged anyone younger to match their skill and stamina. Then they immediately set about confounding their steps with rum, beer, whiskey and gin. Mabouya walked over to the short, heavyset man with the pendulous lower lip, and the bulbous nose that supported glasses with such thick lenses that his eyes appeared as a series of concentric white rings. He stood up with his hand already outstretched.

'So, how are you, old man?' Mabouya greeted him.

'You! Calling me an old man. Look at me. I could outlast any of these dancers,' Humphrey Stephen retorted.

'Yes. Of course,' Mabouya laughed. 'I thought you would be too tired to come so far. Anyway, what's new with you?'

'It's hard when you don't have your own transport. And you ask a favour, and you have to wait until the other person is good and ready,' he explained.

Mabouya nodded. 'So how do you like the dancing? Still good, I think.'

'Yes,' Stephen said, 'and I am glad to see young Christophe is still with you. He is so young ... and already the best dancer in the group. That is strange. But he is so good. Still wants to beat the drum?'

'Uh-huh. I told him he cannot do both. "You're going to dance with the drum between your legs?" I asked him ... but it's more than that ... it is as if something is making him mad for the drum.'

'An obsession with an old drum ...' Stephen said quietly to himself.

'What?' Mabouya asked.

'As if he can't control it?' Stephen replied.

'Yes,' Mabouya nodded. 'Look, he's coming,' he said, pointing with his eyes towards Zaky Christophe.

'M'sieu Mabouya, Mr. Stephen,' Zaky greeted them.

'How are you, Zaky?' they greeted him.

## Chapter 12

# Revelation

Humphrey Stephen had not always had a great interest in country festivals. Twenty years before, he had been an important government official, married to an exotically beautiful girl of nineteen – as his family name and wealth entitled him to. He spent his weekends on his country estate, not sharing in the primitive rituals of his simple neighbours, but entertaining important guests. After one year, his wife left the island with a younger man: a mechanic whose breath did not always stink of cigarettes and rum, and whose lovemaking lasted longer than two minutes. She preferred the mechanic's simple direct declarations of what he wished to do to her body to her husband's interminable and ponderous orations from Shakespeare's sonnets.

Stephen tried joking about losing his wife, pretending that he had left her, but he could not always stop the tears and the tremor in his voice. His important friends left too, some relieved that their own wives had lasted beyond desirability; others envied his unexpected bachelorhood. But they quickly tired of his maudlin self-indulgence, and his aura of failure. He resigned from his job and moved to a small farm in the hills overlooking the capital. His country neighbours were suspicious at first, but when he stopped polishing his shoes, and did not mend his torn clothes, they became more comfortable with him. A widow offered to cook for him, and once a month, she let him persuade her to spend an hour in his bed.

He took up painting again – rural scenes in calm pastels, as if trying to tame the strong bright colours and the hardness of the life around him. Because he did not criticize or denigrate, the country people invited him to their ceremonies and shared secret rituals with him. He would sit calmly through long ceremonies, drinking with them until someone would carry his limp, snoring body to a nearby house. When he asked questions, they were good questions that were always passed on to the oldest people, who in turn – to show their appreciation – would offer long, detailed answers that became minor ceremonies in themselves.

He began to love the old things that had come with the Africans and the Caribs. As he understood them better, he recorded them in thick green ledgers. He began attending meetings of the archaeological society, and slowly received some recognition as an expert on the folklore of the island. The members of the scholarly fraternities forgot to invite him to their homes, but included him on expeditions to dig into the earth for knowledge and potsherds because he had learned from the country people the locations of old Carib villages and refuse pits. He became increasingly uncomfortable in the city, in old worn clothes, and among old friends irritated by his disinterest in their important new acquisitions. Who cared about the gentle respect that he received in the small towns and villages, where he did not have to compete with university graduates and owners of stock certificates?

One day, the parish priest of Rocher sent word asking him to visit. He took the five o'clock morning bus to Rocher and six hours later sat with the old Frenchman in a termite-hollowed, dusty study. The priest swallowed his small brandy quickly and waited politely but impatiently for Stephen to finish his. 'Can you read old French?' the priest asked, when he thought he had waited long enough.

'I don't know ... is it more difficult than the poetry of Ronsard?' he laughed.

'At least the poetry was printed,' the priest smiled. 'This is handwritten but legible. It is the notebook of a priest who lived on the island about two hundred years ago. L'Abbé Joubert. It is very strange ... very, very strange. I expect you will treat this with some confidence: it is the property of the Church. You understand? Give it back as soon as you have read it. And, Monsieur Stephen, do not copy it.'

'I won't copy it,' Stephen promised, almost frightened to take the notebook of brown pages bound in cracked blackened leather that the priest held out.

When the serious business of the morning was done, they went to sit on the balcony to exchange news and shake their heads in sorrow at the latest scandals in the city, reminding each other of how much better it used to be in colonial times. Stephen returned home on the two o'clock bus.

He forgot to sleep that night, and stayed up until three o'clock in the morning with the notebook and a French dictionary. He read of Abbé Joubert's visits to the hills above Rocher, of the ceremonies he had witnessed, and of his friend Ayo, the Yoruba priest. And he read of the Carib drummer – a man named Mabouya, with a large drum covered with hairless grey skin. 'They whisper that the skin is of a human ...' the priest had written. There were illustrations of the drum and the animals carved around it. Stephen could discern camels, lions, elephants, antelopes and crocodiles.

Eventually, his vision blurred with tiredness and Stephen reluctantly gave up, locked the book in a cabinet and went to lie on his bed. But his thoughts kept him awake until the irrepressible calls of the neighbourhood cocks made sleep impossible.

When the widow's coffee made it possible for him to see and think again, he took the notebook out and pored over the pages anew. There were references to the village of Tambour, a man named François, an intimidating woman named Maimouna, and an unusually handsome man who was the best dancer in the village. There were many references to Ayo and Mabouya, the two characters who had drawn the priest back to the hills for repeated visits. There was mention of the death of Ayo, and there were notes for a letter to his superior asking that the Church take an interest in preserving the customs of the blacks. Finally, there were sketches of indigenous vegetables and fruits, each labelled with its Carib name.

## Chapter 13

# Time to leave

Humphrey Stephen complimented Zaky on his dancing. 'Very good, Zaky. These feet of yours must have wings,' he said.

'You think so, Mr. Stephen?' Zaky replied, with the disarming earnestness that left admirers wondering whether Zaky was unaware of his dancing skills.

'Yes . . . yes . . . of course,' Stephen assured him; then smiled at how easily he had been led into prolonging the praise. 'So what are you planning to do with yourself?' he continued.

Zaky paused, looked quickly at Mabouya, and said hesitantly, 'I'm learning how to play the drum. I am trying to copy M'sieu Mabouya. But he won't let me play the old drum.'

'You have your own drum,' Mabouya reminded him.

'M'sieu Mabouya!' Zaky retorted in towering amazement, 'You're comparing my little piece of drum to yours?'

Mabouya chuckled, and glanced at Stephen as if for help. 'This boy wants to make me mad. Go and play with the girls, Zaky. Go, before they come and drag you away.'

Zaky grinned, and as he turned to leave, Stephen held his arm. 'I want to talk to you. I'll stop by next time I'm in Rocher. It's a long time since I climbed Manuage. Take care of yourself.'

'Yes, Mr. Stephen. Walk well,' Zaky replied, and he moved to submerge himself in a tide of devotees.

His retinue moved towards the surrounding food stalls that were almost hidden by discharges of greasy smoke from frying, roasting, barbecuing, grilling and burning chicken, pork and *acras*. Zaky gorged on *acras* and *pain maïs*, the sweet spiced cake of corn meal, coconut, and pumpkin boiled in a banana leaf, and as dense and heavy as a lead sinker – too delectable to eat in moderation. Much later, searing indigestion came to lie in bed with him, to plunge him into nightmare after nightmare, and make him resolve – once again – never to let anything but coconut-water pass his lips for the rest of his life.

Humphrey Stephen visited Zaky's home two months later. He walked in through the open door without knocking, startling Ma Charlotte, who was busy blending vanilla and nutmeg into eggnog with a swizzle stick. 'Mr. Stephen!' she called out in surprise, 'But how are you? You should have told us you were coming, I would have made a little something for you to eat.'

'Thanks, Ma Charlotte, but I'm on my way to Tambour. I passed to see if Zaky can come with me,' Stephen answered. He paused, wondering about Ma Charlotte's silence, then realized he had forgotten to ask about her health, and that of her sons, and the state of things in the village. 'So how are you feeling these days? And the boys? And the children?'

A little mollified, Ma Charlotte gave a brief account of her latest life-threatening illnesses, admitting they were consequences of being alive, and assuring him that she expected to survive with God's grace.

'God is love,' Stephen agreed, thanking Ma Charlotte graciously for darkening his eggnog with too much brandy.

'Zaky is behind there with a neighbour . . . Sylvie,' she informed him, indicating with her thumb. 'I'll call him.' She leaned out of the window and shouted, 'Za-ky-y-y!'

'Okay!' Zaky answered, and they heard a female voice asking him to hurry back.

'Eh! Mr. Stephen,' Zaky greeted his visitor, and they exchanged notes on their health. Ma Charlotte took the opportunity to point out a few ailments she had omitted, asking Zaky to provide confirmation of her diagnosis and of her stoicism in the face of so many burdens.

When it was polite to suggest leaving, and despite Ma Charlotte's protests that he had only just arrived, Stephen asked Zaky to walk with him to Tambour. Zaky persuaded a friend to drive them to the end of the road the government had built halfway to Tambour. The road ended abruptly two miles from the village, as if its builders had suddenly been called away to do more urgent things. A wide path continued up the hillside through fields of orange, purple, and white ground orchids that grew only in the cool damp places near the clouds. Stephen bent to point at a white orchid. 'See that orchid? *Epidendrum nocturnum*,' he said.

Zaky looked at the orchid, '*Epidendrum nocturnum,*' he repeated. 'Something to do with the night?' he asked.

'Yes,' Stephen said. 'It has the nicest perfume ... but puts it out only at night ... probably for some night moth.'

'Um-hm,' Zaky agreed.

The village children saw the visitors, and brought the news long before Zaky and Stephen arrived. The greetings were ready.

'So, how are you? And your brothers? And Ma Charlotte? How is the dancing? Well, you know how it is. God will provide. What to do? Life is hard. When are you getting married?'

'Mr. Stephen! We hardly see you now. You must come and see us more often. You know so-and-so is dead? Yes ... died in his sleep. We will always miss him ... um-hm ... such a good man. So, how are you?'

'So what brought you to see us? And even to bring Zaky with you?'

'Oh, it's been a long time ... time for some good fresh air. And I wanted to see Mabouya,' Stephen said.

'Ah, but yes, he's over by Chilby's house. Chilby has been pooping for a whole week ... nonstop,' someone said.

The crowd laughed, and waited for Stephen to ask for an explanation, but the old man appeared to be distracted.

There was no room for pauses and silences. That would show disinterest. So they had the questions ready – to be asked, answered and repeated. 'Remember to stop by before you leave,' each one said, not quite an invitation, but a reminder to maintain the connections.

'Yes, Yes,' the visitor always promised.

'Good. Walk well,' they wished the visitor.

Mabouya was sitting on the wooden bench-step at the front of his house waiting for them. 'So you're here,' he said in greeting.

Then they settled down to speak. Occasionally, other men from the village would join in. Stephen wanted to continue work on a small dictionary of Carib words for local animals and plants. In return, he told of the latest things he had learned from the magazines and books at the city library.

'So, what's wrong with Chilby?' Stephen asked Mabouya.

But before the latter could answer, one of the villagers, unable to withstand the pain of listening to another tell a good story, spoke up quickly. 'Last Saturday,' he began, 'Chilby came from the city with a bottle of brown liquid he said was '*bois bandé*'. Said a little bit could keep a man hard for hours. We didn't believe him, but all of us wanted to try it. Chilby wouldn't give anybody a drop. Not even for money.'

The speaker paused to look at a companion. 'Eh! Charlo. Didn't your wife try to get some for you?'

Charlo scowled. 'Leave me out of your shit,' he said.

The speaker continued. 'Well, Chilby drank the whole bottle. But he didn't touch his wife. No sir. Not once! Instead, the bastard spent four days in the toilet shitting. Between his groans, we could hear him saying, "Ay! *Bon Dieu*, please don't let me die." By the third day he was begging, "Please don't let me live!" But he didn't die. Don't ever mention *bois bandé* in his presence . . . he'll go crazy.'

Later, after emptying two bottles of Napoleon brandy and a quart of dark rum to show their approval of the day's proceedings, the meeting ended to give Zaky and Stephen time to get back to the main road before darkness fell. Everyone thought they were sure to get a ride back to Mahôt.

Before they left, Stephen took Mabouya's arm and led him out of earshot of the others. 'My friend,' he said, 'I had the strangest experience the other day. If I hadn't seen for myself, I wouldn't be telling you about this. But . . . you know the parish priest. Well, he asked me to come see him about something very important. Told me not to discuss it with anybody. And I agreed, but I feel I have to tell you this. He let me have a look at an old, old document he found in the church records. Let me ask you quickly before my courage leaves. Did you know an Abbé Joubert?'

For what seemed several minutes to Stephen, Mabouya fixed him with unblinking eyes. 'Have you told anyone else about this?' Mabouya asked.

'Nobody,' Stephen answered.

'Good,' Mabouya said. 'But you must hurry up, it's getting dark. Another time . . . not now, we'll talk about this thing. But not now . . . not now.'

Stephen nodded and turned to go. He was covered in sweat. Later, as they walked down the path among the orchids, Stephen turned to Zaky. 'You know why I asked you to come with me to Tambour?'

'Well, it's a long way to come alone,' Zaky answered.

'Oh, I don't mind that,' Stephen said. 'But, you see, you were the youngest person there. In a few years, those like me will be too old to climb up and down these hills to tell stories, and to dance, and remember the old ways. Young people don't have time for these things. I want you to go back to school, Zaky, then go on to university. You are smart. You have talent. These people know you.'

'I know, that's why I'm with the dance group,' Zaky answered.

'Yes, yes,' he persisted, 'but if you don't go to university, people will just see you as the handsome country boy who can dance better than anybody else. But you won't have the respect. People will only listen if you have something behind your name. That's how it is, Zaky . . . you know that.'

Zaky was silent for so long that Stephen wondered whether he had offended him. 'Zaky?' he said, concerned.

'I'm okay . . . I was thinking,' Zaky answered, 'but what'm I going to study? Dancing? And how am I going to pay for it?'

'Oh, come on, Zaky! You're smart. Look, you're only twenty. Think about it. Talk to your brothers. I know your father would have wanted you to go on. Take my advice, go to university.'

They walked on in silence. Zaky was already missing the sights and sound of the hills before he had even decided to go to university.

After they arrived at Mahôt, Zaky asked his brother Mark to drive Stephen to the presbytery in Rocher, where he would spend the night with the parish priest before taking the early morning bus to the capital. For several minutes, Zaky stood looking at the bend in the road where Mark's van had disappeared. He moved backwards and, without looking, sat on the steps at the front of the house. He tried to understand how an invitation to accompany Humphrey Stephen to Mahôt had ended with him agreeing to go back to school. And university! Zacharias Christophe, B.A. Crazy shit!

He discussed it over and over with his brothers and his dance-group director. They listened, frowned painfully at the ground, and said, 'Go.'

Ma Charlotte was overjoyed at first, then burst into tears – as if her youngest son had suddenly revealed his intention to leave immediately for the remotest Pacific island.

'But, Ma, I'm only going back to my old school. In Rocher. And only for a year,' he protested.

'I know, but I'll be alone in the house now,' she complained.

'Well, I've got to leave someday. And the others aren't far away,' he answered.

Matthew drove Zaky to Rocher. His teachers welcomed him back, especially Miss Rosalie Justin, the English teacher who had had to rely on fading memories of this body and face to nourish her fantasies.

Two years later, to Zaky's avowed elation, but secret disappointment, he passed the university entrance examinations. Humphrey Stephen set out at once to ensure that Zaky committed himself to going to university before the drum reminded him of the cold loneliness of studying abroad. The old man asked to visit a government official whom he still considered a friend. The friend listened seriously, and said he would do what he could to help Zaky. He did not expect Stephen to return the favour: the old man had nothing but goodwill in sufficient quantity to share with anyone. Yes, he would talk with Zaky and see what he could do to help. 'Goodbye, Mr. Stephen. The country needs resources like young Christophe. You know I'll do what I can,' he said, as Stephen walked out of his office, leaving a faint, afterimage of poverty and failure that sent a small shiver through the official.

One month later, Zaky received a letter from the Department of Education expressing pleasure in his application for a scholarship to pursue further study in the United Kingdom. Zaky had not made such an application, but thought it impolite to write back and say so. He assumed that had come from Stephen's effort.

Zaky's grades gained him acceptance to London University, where – in obligation to Humphrey Stephen – he would study economics and history, on a scholarship provided by the government. His family would have to supplement the small stipend: the Ministry of Education did not provide for such luxuries as food and clothing. In return, the government expected him to put his skills to the benefit of his country in a 'capacity commensurate with his qualifications.'

The words on the many documents he was asked to sign were devoid of the lightheartedness of the officials who handed them to him. The important people studied his signature, nodded approvingly, then applied themselves to festooning the papers with billows of signatures.

The news of Zaky's triumph flew among the villages of Manuage and Rocher. Relatives brought him essentials like pillows and boxes of dried meat and vegetables. They gave him enough towels to soak up most of the Caribbean Sea. Bed linen came in large amounts and many colours. His aunts and female cousins immediately began crying in preparation for the deluge to come on the day of his departure. The week before he left, he visited every neighbour and relative, and they made him promise to come and say goodbye on his last day, each one hoping for the honour of being the last to speak to him. 'Um-hm,' they would say, 'he made sure to spend his last night by us, you know.' And they would shake their heads as if to say they did not deserve such consideration – such a caring boy.

The last neighbour he said goodbye to was Sylvie Khodra. She was the daughter of an itinerant East Indian merchant who had arrived in Mahôt on a Saturday afternoon, nineteen years earlier, pushing an old Raleigh bicycle loaded with clothes for sale.

After Arvid Khodra had sold half of his cargo, he sat on a fallen log and looked at the hills around him and at the sea that shone between their peaks. He wore an expression of one who had at last been able to sit after a immense journey. Near nightfall, he knocked at Ma Charlotte's door and asked whether she would accept payment for letting him spend the night. Ma Charlotte gave him supper and laid a small straw mattress on the floor of the small sitting-room. She laughed at his offer to pay, and he did not press the matter. The next day he thanked her profusely and asked whether anyone had a small property for sale. One month later, Matthew Christophe sold him half an acre of rocky land, on which he built a house with a shop next door.

With the same decisiveness, he courted and married a distant cousin of Ma Charlotte. She bore him two sons and a daughter in three years. He adored the little girl, and would have given her wings if he could, so that her feet need never touch the ground.

Sylvie looked like both her parents at once. From her mother, she got her always-pursed lips that made those who did not know her wait expectantly for her to speak; and the nose, skewed slightly to the left, gave her face a delicate uncertainty that men turned around to see again. Her father gave his large brown eyes and thick graceful brows, and the plump cheeks that unfailingly launched the pinches of old ladies who came to the shop.

Zaky never became used to Sylvie's appeal, and it both intimidated and comforted him. She let Zaky have almost everything that he wanted from her. But she would not sleep with him; and he never dared to ask until the night before he left for England. With tears pouring down her cheeks, she shook her head. No.

'But I may not see you again . . . . ' Zaky protested. 'You may get married. *I* may get married.'

Sylvie shook her head and buried her face in Zaky's shoulder. Zaky said goodbye, feeling like a malefactor beyond the reach of confession and absolution.

*Chapter 14*

# The hardening place

August fourteenth, 1972. The flight to London was Zaky's first encounter with an aeroplane. He crossed the Atlantic Ocean and travelled all the way to Heathrow Airport without once shutting his eyes in sleep, afraid that he would miss some small unravelling of the miracle of aeronautics.

In later years, he could not recall boarding the aeroplane, whether he had used the bathroom, or whether he had spoken to another passenger. His sharpest recollection was the embarrassment of collecting the contents of his broken suitcase from the luggage carousel.

He had written to the friend of a relative asking whether someone could meet him at the airport, but the friend had not replied. But when he left the customs and immigration hall, his eye caught the hand-held sign that said: 'ZACHARIAS CHRISTOPHE'.

'Sorry I didn't write. Should have. But here you are,' his welcomer said. 'Name's Coll. Good flight?'

'Yes,' Zaky said. 'Is it morning or afternoon? Can't see the sun.'

'Bit overcast all week,' Coll said. 'It's morning. Sun won't set 'til night. Bit disturbing at first, but you'll like it. Winter's dark . . . all day.'

Coll led him outside to the taxi rank. 'Got your address in London? Good. Take a black cab there.'

Zaky would not recall much of his ride to his student hall of residence either, but he managed to keep his eyes open often enough to marvel at the precise lines and curves of lawns along the highway. He wondered whether the grass was cropped one blade at at time and whether the green carpets were ever defiled by weeds.

And the buildings: massive and sombre. Like limestone extrusions whose surfaces had been carved and sculpted to simulate arrangements of blocks and columns. Roads as wide as the runway of the airport near his country's capital. No sounds of horns; no calls of greeting; no sounds of birds or dogs. Just a heavy thrumming as if the city sat on the skin of an immeasurable drum. And soft voices that sent words only as far as a companion's ear. Nothing familiar.

No smells of fruit or the sea or smoke or people. Only the stink of gasoline and diesel fumes; and wet wool . . . like sheep in the rain.

'What d'you think of London?' Coll asked.

'What did you think when you arrived?' Zaky replied.

'Same as you: cold and dark. Wanted to ask the taxi to turn around.'

'Know what you mean.' Zaky said.

'Good to know it's always too late to do that. But you'll cheer up when the sun comes out again. Still some time for that to happen before the winter.' But when he saw Zaky's frown, he added, 'Just joking. You'll be all right after a nap.'

When he looked around, he could not find the edges of the city: no hills or ocean horizons. 'So damn big,' he remembered saying.

No recollections again until he woke in a small room on a couch that doubled as a bed. There was a wash-basin to the left of the door and a window at the opposite end. There was a note under his door.

> *Welcome to London again. When you're alive again, take a walk to Madame Tussaud's or the Zoo. Also you're not far from Baker Street of Sherlock Holmes fame. If you walk south along Baker Street (left from your residence) you'll eventually come to Oxford Street. That's interesting – nice stores. Do take time to visit Piccadilly Circus and Speakers' Corner. Lots of fun. My 'phone no. is at the bottom. Call sometime. In a couple months you may even get to like the place. Much to do. Don't forget the theatre – best in the world. Coll.*

The next day he telephoned Coll, but there was no answer. He called one more time, then lost the number. He never saw him again.

He visited the Zoo the next morning and discovered that the animals whose pictures he had seen in books were much larger than he had imagined. In the afternoon he visited Madame Tussaud's. That was the first thing he would mention when he returned: how he had said 'Excuse me,' to a guard at the top of the stairs, only to find out that he had spoken to a wax statue – a mistake that others made too. Then he would tell them an elephant was as tall as a house, and a rhinoceros was a long as a car.

At breakfast, he made his first friend: a Norwegian student who had arrived two days before. She brought her breakfast tray to his table. She extended her hand and introduced herself. 'Margaja,' she said.

She agreed to help him find Piccadilly Circus. On his first Friday evening, they sat on the steps surrounding the statue of Eros and watched groups of tired, homesick Americans resting from their search for a restaurant that sold hamburgers and Cokes. The colonisation of London's streets by McDonald's had not yet begun.

The first letters from home arrived after two weeks. His mother wrote to tell him over and over how they missed him and how they expected wonderful things from him. She listed all the relatives and neighbours who sent their regards. And she reminded him to attend Church. He promised himself that in his next letter he would tell her that he did, and how different it was from home. Before he left London, he did visit St. Paul's Cathedral. That was the only time he entered a place of worship during his stay in England.

He did not open Sylvie's letter as eagerly as he had anticipated. He had begun forgetting her face; and the sound of her voice coming with the words on the perfumed paper did not belong to this place with its sharp-edged accents. He stopped reading her later letters, finding her simple enquiries and sentiments uncomfortable intrusions in an environment of polished speech and learned dissertations. He stopped writing. Threw her unopened letters into the wastebasket. He was relieved when her letters stopped coming. But he still missed her – as one misses comfortable but discarded things. Missed her when loneliness came – and hurt.

He saw Margaja almost every day. Together they learned how to travel on the London Underground, and how to hop on and off double-decker buses with appropriate nonchalance and disregard for the conductors' warnings.

One Saturday afternoon, she asked him to accompany her to a jeweller's near Piccadilly Circus. She handed a note to a salesman, who then asked them to accompany him into an inner room. Another man came in with two trays of jewellery, which he spread delicately on pads of black velvet. Margaja asked Zaky to help her pick three bracelets and three necklaces of gold and emeralds. The jeweller wrapped the pieces in tissue and put them into velour bags that he closed with draw strings. Margaja signed a receipt. The jeweller rose. Margaja handed the bags to Zaky. 'Pockets,' she said to Zaky, patting the front of her thighs. He stuffed the bags into his front pockets. He trembled all the way back to the residence; wished he had written to Sylvie; wondered whether mental confession of his sins would suffice to save his soul if he were to be robbed and murdered on the bus.

When they made it back to the hall of residence without incident, he was surprised and slightly disappointed that they had not been held up at gunpoint. 'To your room,' Margaja ordered.

In his room, she retrieved the jewellery from Zaky and tossed the pieces carelessly on to the sheet of his unmade bed. Zaky looked on uncertainly as she flopped down on to the pillow and began lazily fingering a necklace with a look that was both admiring and dismissive.

'Beautiful, yes?' she said, dropping the necklace again and stretching back on the bed. 'Ever made love on a bed worth sixty thousand pounds?'

Zaky stared at her open mouthed. 'Sixty thousand pounds! You made me carry sixty thousand pounds in my pockets? On a train? Are you mad? What if we'd been robbed?'

Margaja sat up, laughing hard. 'Do you think you look like someone carrying gold and emeralds? On the Central Line! Oh Zaky, you're perfect – the jewellery was safer in your pocket than in an armoured car.' And seeing his expression – quivering between fury and comic appreciation – another ripple of laughter escaped her throat and flushed her face. 'Come here,' she said, stretching out her arm towards him, 'and let me make it better.'

Zaky hesitated, still feeling that he had been endangered, or at least manipulated. Margaja stood up and put her arms round him. 'I guess I really should pay my guard . . . my hero,' she said. 'It's only fair.'

They made love on the most expensive bedcovers in London, but Zaky did not enjoy it as much as he had imagined he would when he had fantasized about her at other times – without the cold sharp clutter of her glittering aphrodisiacs.

When they had finished, he asked, 'Are you going to wear all this stuff?'

'No, no. I smuggle it back to Oslo . . . as my personal things.'

Zaky looked intensely at her, but could make nothing out: her voice seemed to come from another world. He felt uneasy, guilty even – not at his 'infidelity' to Sylvie, which was excusable in a city of such monstrous temptations, but because he felt somehow that he had been sucked into some unseemly, underworld, currents, and he didn't want to swim in that sea however voluptuous and obliging the company.

He tried to avoid her the following week, excusing himself by saying that he had to revise for some examinations. She was not put off, but remained as friendly as before. Yet the impression that he had been used persisted with Zaky. They did make love once more, one night a week or so later, but Zaky insisted they turn the light off. He did not want to see the bedsheets and be reminded of cold, hard, uncomfortable pieces of green and gold.

One morning, a month later, she told him that she was pregnant. 'But I didn't . . .' he began to plead.

'Sh!' she interrupted. 'It's not yours. It's my boyfriend's. He's coming over from Oslo soon – to decide what to do.' She looked at her hands absently. 'I'm not sure I can manage with a baby now. But when it's over, I can see you again. Yes?'

There was an almost naive trust in her voice that deflected his anger for the moment and so he just muttered something inconsequential like, 'Of course. Yes, I understand how it is.'

For the rest of the day, he found little comfort and barely any distraction in a full programme of classes. His attention was elsewhere – he may have escaped becoming a father, but he had not escaped becoming a fool.

On his way home by bus later that afternoon, a conductor with an east European accent examined his monthly card and found something to say about, 'You people . . .' And to complete his day, a man wearing a thick black woollen coat brushed past him, pushing Zaky off the pavement into the traffic. He said something Zaky did not understand, but echoes of the words stayed in the air, joining with the heavy smell of stale burned grease from the man's coat, and the musty smell of damp basements.

When Zaky got back to his room, he rushed into the bathroom to vomit; then he sat on his bed to fill his mind with memories of Sylvie. He tried hard to miss her again when Margaja joined him for dinner. He went to bed choking with angry humiliation, which he considered to be punishment for his abandonment of Sylvie. He even thought of returning home. But how to explain to his family that he had been humiliated by a rich Norwegian girl? The village would laugh for a lifetime.

He was lying in bed, far from sleep, rehearsing vengeful things he could visit on Margaja, when the room suddenly filled with the smell of turned soil, wet leaves and wood smoke. He heard the dry rasping voice, like the flutter of pages that had not been turned in centuries: 'Walk well, son of . . .'

He had heard, but not understood the last word; it sounded like 'doom.' He lay trembling violently, his forehead already damp, and whispered, 'M'sieu Mabouya?' After a few seconds, he smiled at the absurdity of his words and went to the door. There was no one in the hallway. He went back to bed, assuming that he had fallen asleep after all, and had been dreaming. The next morning, he decided to end his relationship with Margaja with whatever fragments of dignity he could salvage.

The following weekend, he attended a performance of Kafka's *Metamorphosis*, and afterwards, in a state of profound depression turned left on Tottenham Court Road and walked along Oxford Street to Hyde Park. No one had looked at him. It was exactly as he had thought: in that city, one metamorphosed into objects visible only when it was convenient – for ferrying jewellery, for instance. Even the whelk-seller in Portobello Market who called him 'ducks' did so out of habit to all her customers. Without her whelks and his money, he would be invisible to her. When he made it back to his rooms two and a half hours later, his feet burned as if he had walked on live embers. Despite his exhaustion, he made no attempt to go to bed, afraid of the thrumming of the city that he felt through the walls: like great hands beating upon the surface of the world.

He went to his desk and wrote a long affectionate letter to Sylvie. She would never reply.

He wrote to his mother regularly, although she seldom wrote back; and complained, when she did, that he did not write often enough. Humphrey Stephen wrote every month, whether Zaky did or not. His letters listed the new activities or projects that were planned or contemplated or in progress, and in which he thought Zaky should become involved and make important contributions. There were, for example, recent excavations of Amerindian middens and burial grounds. These had been done under the supervision of world-famous experts from Berlin and New York, and had provided hitherto unsuspected information about the original inhabitants of the island. Of course, great care had been taken to ensure that the skeletons had been replaced, and the sites concealed. But always, there were his concerns about the lack of scholarship and integrity in the new breed of politicians. 'But these are the eternal complaints of the old about the young,' the letters explained. So Zaky was not disturbed by Stephen's news.

In three years Zaky obtained his degree, and did so with such ease that his Economics professor suggested that he apply for a postgraduate course. He wrote to the Ministry of Education requesting an extension of his scholarship, hoping they would refuse, but their reply ordered him to apply to graduate school.

In his fourth year in London, Zaky obtained a greater measure of comfort than he had felt before in London. This was due mostly to weekend visits he paid to his new friend whom he met at a party. Her name was Anemony – 'with-a-Y, love' – Dennison. A nurse who was a divorced mother of two, she had come with her parents from the Caribbean when she was seven months old. She did not say which year, and in all the time he knew her, Zaky never discovered her exact age – although she repeatedly reminded him of her birthday.

Anemony was not as pretty as he usually liked his women to be, but she reminded him immediately of those graceful black singers who all seemed to come from Detroit and whose voices were shaped and tuned by church choirs. He was immediately seduced by the warm dark fragrance of her voice, which too was spiced with rich gospel notes.

After their first thirty minutes of conversation, she insisted that he come and visit her at her flat in Kentish Town. She said she did not have much company, and thought it would be super for both of them if Zaky could visit occasionally for tea and a chat – while her daughter and son were out with their father. And if he didn't feel like making small talk, they could just sit and watch the telly. He didn't have to bring anything. 'Got a bottle of the best plonk in the 'fridge, she promised, laughing.

Lonely. Like him. Wanted to hear voices other than her children's. Wanted to be touched by someone still not too familiar. Like him. They made love the first time he visited – on the couch in her living-room, and she reacted with such violent enthusiasm that Zaky wondered aloud why he had been so blessed.

'Most chaps don't want to muck about with a girl who's got kids . . . well, the nice ones don't, anyway,' Anemony explained.

'So what did you do before this? Abstain?' he asked.

'I see an old friend once a month,' she replied.

'Anyone I know?' he asked, trying to sound casual although her explanation had pricked him a little.

'Cor! But you're nosey for a first-timer, aren't you, love?' she laughed.

'Okay, Okay,' Zaky laughed back, recognizing how ridiculous it was for him to be jealous and also afraid that he was beginning to irritate her.

Anemony rose to go to the bathroom. When she returned, still naked, she was holding up two expensive-looking black dresses. 'Like?' she asked.

'They're nice, I suppose,' Zaky said. 'Don't know much about dresses.'

'They are, and pretty expensive too. I couldn't afford them.'

'So?' Zaky asked, his face beginning to burn uncomfortably from what he expected to be an unpleasant disclosure.

Anemony held the dresses up to her chin. 'Once a month, I go to see this old blighter . . . friend of mine. Owns a dress shop in Islington. Married, but his wife's more interested in the telly and her cats. So . . . so, I act out his fantasies. The horny old bastard can get up to some pretty odd things, but . . . sometimes he actually gets it up. 'Course, I don't ever laugh at him. Tell him it's okay . . . shouldn't worry. So, he tells me to pick something off the racks. Puts it down to shoplifting, I s'pose. I don't ever take anything too expensive . . . just nice. Keeps both of us happy.' She looked closely at Zaky. 'Thought I was a nice girl, eh?'

'No, no! It's not that at all. I think it's . . . I think it's . . . well, I think it's . . . fine. And I really have no business getting into your affairs. But I was . . . a little . . . jealous.'

'Not to worry, love, you've already been there,' Anemony laughed.

'Where?' he frowned.

'In my affairs, ducky, my very private affairs . . . in me . . . you know . . .' she said, directing her eyes towards her lap.

He grinned, and rose to take the dresses from her. He laid them on the couch. Then he pushed her down to the floor, and they made love again.

Afterwards, there did not seem too many important things to say, so Zaky turned on the television. 'Let's have a look at *The Avengers*. Maybe Mrs. Peel's going to let Steed have a go.'

Zaky's affair with Anemony gave a routine to his life that enabled him to study without the distractions of romantic expeditions. She would be there for him whenever he wanted – except one day a month. But he assuaged his jealousy of the storeowner by convincing himself that it was the older man who was the cuckold.

One Saturday evening, he arrived at her flat and was surprised to find the children at home.

'Their father's gone out of town,' she explained. 'But it's all right. We can sit and watch the telly. Or listen to the stereo, if you like.'

Later, when the children had ben put to bed, they abandoned caution. They were entwined about each other on the couch when the door opened suddenly. They looked up to see the boy standing in the doorway. He was staring at their naked bodies, making little hoarse squeaking sounds as if he were trying to force unendurable screams past his constricted throat.

Zaky sat up terrified. Anemony quickly slipped on her skirt and walked to the door. She took the child's hand and led him out, closing the door behind her. Zaky dressed hurriedly and was considering stealing out, when Anemony returned.

'It's all right,' she said, 'he's autistic. Doesn't understand what he saw . . . I don't think. I told him we were playing. He's fine now. Are you going?'

'Thought I should,' Zaky said. 'Didn't know what was happening.'

'No, don't go, love . . . not before we . . . finish,' she said.

She coaxed Zaky into undressing again, but the memory of the disturbed, frantic child standing in the lighted doorway defeated his best intentions.

And for the remainder of his stay in London, he refused to make love in her flat. She had to go to his residence, where his fellow students would set up a guard of honour along the hallway to welcome the smartly dressed Anemony as she walked arm in arm with her admirably nonchalant escort. They both enjoyed the brief celebrity her visits gave them. She would stride down the hallway, exaggerating the swing of her hips, provoking envious fantasies from his neighbours. Zaky imagined them with their ears pressed against the walls next to his room, and so he and Anemony learned to stifle their instincts and conduct their affair in frustrating silence.

She never made unreasonable emotional demands on him. And there were times when he thought he loved her: when she did things for him with no expectation of return; or warmed his toes on winter nights when they itched mercilessly from chilblains.

When the old nightmares came, he imagined Anemony holding his face, and the loss of the drum became less important. Soon the nightmares stopped altogether. Sometimes he toyed with the thought of asking her to marry him. Then, he imagined her response: 'Well, fancy that! Me and two kids, and you being a university scholar and all. Wouldn't do, love. But ta very much.' That solved the problem; no need to ask.

Zaky remained in London for one month after his graduation, to see the things that visitors came to see, but which residents put off until some other time because they would always be there. He went almost as a kind of duty because he knew that back home, they would ask about these places: Buckingham Palace, Westminster Abbey, the Tower of London, Big Ben, London Bridge – is it still falling? So he went. He took Anemony to the Tate Gallery and was pleased when she recognized Rodin's *The Kiss*.

'Bloody hell . . . it's rough,' she commented. 'Not like in the pictures. Must have been a pretty good kisser to keep her staying all twisted like that.'

Too loud. Several visitors giggled while Zaky pretended great interest in the marble's pitted surface.

He was happier when he took her to a dance club for the first time. But afterwards, in the bright light of the club's foyer, he saw that her eyes were swollen with crying.

'What's wrong?' he asked.

'Gonna miss you something awful,' she said.

'I'll miss you too, Anemony,' he said, trying hard to sound sufficiently wretched.

'Bollocks!' she said, and was silent all the way home in the cab, while he hid his shame by staring through the window at shopfronts and the vague ripples of neon promises. Like his own promises. London had hardened him, exchanging some of his vulnerability for cynicism.

He spent his last night in London with Anemony. Both were subdued and they watched television in virtual silence, neither stimulated by the canned laughter of a popular situation comedy into laughing themselves. As they sat together on the couch, Anemony occasionally turned to look at Zaky, but he stared fixedly at the screen as if willing it to vacuum out of him all his memories, all his regrets.

Later, they made love, but neither had to stifle any cries for there were none. Between them was an unspoken sadness that expressed itself in the langour of their movements, and each made love as if performing a last rite for the other.

She rose early to make him breakfast, and to call a taxi. When the doorbell rang, she would not accompany him to the door, but remained seated on the couch, staring unblinkingly at the wall. She tried bravely to smile when he kissed her goodbye, but the tears ran into her mouth.

'Write,' she managed to say.

As his plane lifted off, already his recollections of her, and of his entire stay in London, were becoming as hazy and remote as the view from his seat.

## Chapter 15

# The strangeness of home

They came by the busload to meet him. Relatives, friends and neighbours dressed in Sunday clothes filled the terminal building; and visitors stood on tiptoe, craning their necks and readying cameras for the unknown celebrity.

Zaky could see the crowd milling in the viewers' gallery and wondered about the dignitary who was leaving. He had seen no indication that anyone especially important had been a fellow passenger. He joined the line of stiff-legged and rumpled passengers obediently following an airline attendant to the arrival lounge. He searched in the crowd for the faces of his mother and brothers. Then he understood what the noise was that he had heard from the steps of the aircraft: they were shouting, 'Zaky! Zaky!'

All those country people. All those colours. All those hands waving to call his attention to one or other expectant face. All that noise. His mortification felt like flaming thorns dragged across his neck and face, and the sweat boiled out of him. He consoled himself with the thought that in a few hours all of this would pass; when, hopefully, the immigration officers, taxi drivers, airport staff, and other onlookers would forget his face. He concentrated on persuading his feet to follow each other in proper sequence, thankful that the two bags he carried precluded any waving. He smiled bravely at the crowd.

Thirty minutes later, he walked slowly into the vast, sodden embrace of his family and the accompanying multitude.

The next day, his family prepared more food than they could eat. They filled the large clay pots called cannaries with yams, green bananas, *dachine*, rice, plantains, eddoes, and breadfruit; and boiled them to such tenderness that pieces had to be scooped up with spoons. Ma Charlotte and her sons' wives perfumed

Latanier with stews of lamb, beef and chicken, cooked in thick brown sauces that sent off vapours rich enough to spread on bread. Smells of onions, chives, thyme, garlic, curry and cinnamon visited everything, sticking to clothes and faces and making the guests as redolent as the filled plates they carried out of the kitchens.

Sylvie Khodra came in the evening with a sponge cake covered in white and pink icing, and bejewelled with enough silver-coloured candy beads to repel the blow of a cleaver. She was followed by a large, tall man, whom Zaky did not recognize, carrying an infant who looked like a miniature of Sylvie. The women crowded around to say how they wished they had Sylvie's baking skills. Zaky gaped with surprise, and forgot to smile when Sylvie introduced her husband.

Zaky bent to kiss her cheek, wanting to say something suitably polite, but his jealousy choked him. He shook hands hurriedly with Corinth.

'Heard a lot about you,' Corinth offered; then succumbed to the smells of food around him, and headed for a laden table.

'Well, let me go and help,' Sylvie smiled. Then her lower lip trembled. 'You didn't write,' she said into his ear, and walked away, leaving Zaky with the taste of face powder, vanilla, and almond on his lips.

People came from as far away as Tambour to see Zaky – the first resident of Manuage to earn two university degrees. Everyone asked to see the documents, and Zaky had to explain repeatedly that the university would send them to him in a few weeks. Several older people complained about the inevitable little faults of great institutions. Of course, Mabouya did not come, but this was not unexpected or resented.

For three days, Zaky was ferried up hill, down hill, through forests, across bridges, and along narrow paths to revisit those who had not been able to come to Mahôt to welcome him home.

The homecoming did not give Zaky the joy he had wanted. Through all the smiles and his reassurances that he was glad to be home, there was the pain of missing Anemony. He was also disoriented by the closeness of dirt and the smell of mould that grew on everything in the warm, humid climate. He had forgotten the immediacy of scarred faces and rough hands; the rotten teeth and heavy breaths; and the suffocating closeness of people who sat so near that their mingled sweat ran in cold rivulets down his arms, or soaked into his shirt and pants.

It would take him one year to overcome his nostalgia for London.

Eventually, Humphrey Stephen came to visit. The old man shook hands brusquely, and tried to hide his delight over seeing Zaky by declaring matter of factly, 'Got to go see Mabouya soon. He'll be glad to see you.'

Zaky tried but was unable to hide his disaffection with the old Carib. 'I've got so much to do, I don't know when I'll be able to go to Mahôt,' he said.

'But there are things . . . very important things you must hear from . . .' Stephen protested.

'I know,' Zaky interrupted. 'But you know I need to visit the Ministry of Education. Must find out what my situation is. Let me get these things out of the way first. And honestly, I'm exhausted with all the visiting. Haven't had a moment to myself.'

'Yes . . . yes, I understand,' Stephen replied. His disappointment showed.

'Look, Mr. Stephen, just let me get things settled with the ministry,' Zaky said. 'I'm really confused with all the changes. In only five . . . six years.'

'I know . . . I know,' Stephen replied, 'but be careful, some of the changes have not been good. There are strange things happening in the country, Zaky.'

Zaky nodded. He did not know what the 'strange things' were, or how they affected him. Old people hated changes.

## Chapter 16

# Sellers of hillsides

The official who had arranged the scholarship for Zaky – as a favour to Humphrey Stephen – had moved to a new, more luxurious office. He welcomed Zaky with a long, firm handshake that his degrees entitled him to.

'Sit down ... sit down, my friend,' he said, grinning like the host of a visitor who came bearing rare gifts.

'So,' he continued, when he had assured himself that Zaky was sufficiently comfortable, 'we have plans for you. Yes ... yes, lots of big plans. You know, the government is very oriented towards economic development for our people. Eh?'

Zaky nodded.

'Good,' he said. 'Now we have been considering how we will use your talents. Yes ... yes, we had long discussions about you. You see? Here you are, an economist and a man of art and culture. Now, with the big push for tourism, we are going to need you to help guide things along. You understand?'

'I see,' Zaky lied.

'Good ... good,' the official continued, this time beaming as if he were about to give Zaky the secret location of the Holy Grail. 'You will head a new office that will help us utilize our cultural and historical resources for ... how do I say it? For ... greater exposure. Yes ... greater exposure. Let's utilize our resources. Let the tourists see something other than limbo dancers and fire-eaters. Enough of that steelband stuff! Everybody's got the same crap. Eh? Let's give people something different. Enough of the native garb! What d'you think, man ... what d'you think? Unh? Unh?'

The man's earnestness and fervour poured over Zaky like a mudslide.

111

'Yes . . . yes,' Zaky said, trying to join the rush of the official's passion. 'Yes, of course.'

Zaky waited for the official to rub his hands together in satisfaction. But the other clasped his hands behind his head, and leaned back in his chair.

'Today is the eleventh,' he said. 'We would like you to start work next month . . . the first Monday. That's the third. How about that?' Then he reached for the telephone. 'Miss Marais, Mr. Christophe will need to fill out some papers. Can you help him with that? Thanks.'

He then rose to show Zaky to the door, all the time smiling like an uncle who had just spent thirty minutes with his favourite nephew.

Zaky shook hands vigorously again, and left wondering whether he should have tried to say more than he did.

When he had shut the door after Zaky, the official went to his desk and stood before it for a few seconds, wiping the sweat off his hands and forehead; then he picked up the telephone and dialled. 'Just had a talk with the Christophe feller, Sir. Seems okay. We'll treat him well. I think he'll want to help us. Thank you, Sir.'

He put down the telephone gently; and this time, he rubbed his hands together.

A tall, statuesque, and expensively dressed woman met Zaky in the hallway outside the official's office. Zaky guessed that she was five feet, eight inches tall and about his age. Her eyes were grey with flecks of brown and he was fascinated by her brows, which met over her nose, then swept back to her temples. He wanted to say something flattering about the dimple in her left cheek, but decided to leave this to a later time.

'I'm Jenna Marais,' she said, extending her hand. Her voice had a comforting softness, and she leaned forward slightly when she spoke, as if to ensure that Zaky understood every word. Jenna Marais's voice had become slightly hoarse, and she had difficulty breathing, because Zaky's presence made the air too thin around her.

She led Zaky to her office, through a gauntlet of whispers from other women, and little noises of approval: 'Um . . . um . . . ummm.'

Miss Marais's face bore an expression that clearly said, 'This one's mine!'

In her office, Zaky accepted the documents she handed him, pretended to read them and signed where she told him to. He wondered whether others would notice the smell of perfume that her hands, presence and furniture had transferred to him. Zaky tried not to look too long at Jenna Marais; she was beginning to make him think he was committing some sin, just being in the same room as her. He considered asking her to stop caressing her upper lip with the tip of her tongue. This too, he put off for a later date.

Jenna explained that the agreements he had signed provided him with a low-interest loan for the purchase of a car and a government-owned apartment in the city – a 'nice view, quiet, you'll just love it' kind of apartment.

Zaky nodded, and took his copies of the documents he had signed. As he rose to leave, he glanced at her hands, and not seeing a wedding ring, said bravely, 'Maybe you'll be able to visit?'

'An invitation, Mr. Christophe?' Jenna asked.

'Yes,' Zaky replied.

'I'll take it. Thanks,' she said, licked her lip again, and extended her hand to say goodbye. Her perfume stayed on his hand for hours, and throughout the afternoon he would raise it casually to his face for a reminder.

Zaky left shortly afterwards for Mahôt wondering how things could have gone so smoothly; and worried that he had not said something important. He had borrowed Luke's small truck to travel to the city, and it was not until he was halfway home that he noticed the rust that created a chaos of irregular lines and circles on the body of the vehicle. He glanced with distaste at the mud that had bonded over time with the upholstery, and he became impatient with Luke for not being neater. He ignored the children who turned at the sound of his truck, to wave frantically and call for a ride. He left them to shout curses at him for forcing them back to the small strips of grass the road builders had left: occasional relief for their bare feet from the burn of the sun-heated asphalt. Somebody was always demanding a favour.

He longed for the order and quiet of London, where he could walk the city streets without someone calling or waving at him, distracting him from excursions among the eternal mounds of dog droppings on wet pavements. He was tired of his old friends whose conversations – on the rare occasions when they were not embellishing yet another common encounter with yet another simple woman – could not be taken beyond the costs and speeds of new cars. He was tired of his family, too: of his mother who cared for nothing beyond the view of Manuage; of his brothers who derived unflagging contentment in describing in limitless and repeated detail the latest, trite achievements of their dirt-coated, fly-escorted children.

Most of all, he resented the old Carib who had not, even after a month since Zaky's return, sent word asking him to visit. When the old bastard died, he would ensure that the drum would become an article of historical interest – to be left in his safekeeping.

The entire family was relieved when Zaky moved to the city two weeks later. And he did not miss them for a month. Jenna showed him around the city and introduced him to her friends – who all said they had heard good things about him – and helped him arrange the furniture in his new apartment. He had a wide view of the hills north of the city and of the sea. That helped to keep his mind off the slopes of Manuage and the sea at Rocher. He was content with this life.

Jenna invited him to a boat picnic one Sunday. He drove alone to the docks, and after climbing aboard the large yacht, he strolled along the deck smiling tentatively at the few faces he recognized. She was not aboard, and he was considering how to leave the boat without drawing comment, when she drove up in a new Mercedes with a man whose self-assuredness was as unabashed as the hood ornament on his car. Jenna poured herself out of the car, wearing a lemon-coloured, terrycloth outfit with a sleeveless top and matching shorts made to flatter legs that went on forever. The men on the yacht gasped and looked at their companions. The women frowned, and muttered their concerns about sunburn and lack of fashion sense. Zaky wished he had gone to the country to find fault with his family.

He had never been on a large boat before; and his height above the water, and the wallowing motion of the boat made his mouth fill with salty saliva. He was too ill even to notice when two women flirted with him; and another offered to check

114

out his bed at any time – preferably on a Friday or Saturday night. Zaky smiled, refused drinks, ignored offers of companionship, and cursed Jenna.

Eventually, Jenna came over. 'So, enjoying yourself?' she asked Zaky. He stared back in pale rebuttal. Her escort had become involved in a loud, rum-flavoured argument over the working of the yacht's compass: on whether the needle remained stationary, as he insisted, or whether it turned, as a drunk crewman contended. Those guests whose legs and stomachs allowed movement went to take sides in the argument.

'I'm fine,' Zaky said.

Jenna shook her head. 'No sweetheart, you look like you want to throw up. I'm sorry,' she said.

'It's okay,' Zaky protested.

'Well, just don't die on me. Okay?'

Zaky smiled faintly and looked towards the crowd, 'Your boyfriend?' he asked.

Jenna shrugged her shoulders. 'Used to be, but he found out that he wasn't comfortable with women. You know what I'm talking about?' she said.

Zaky nodded. 'I know,' he said.

'But we still go out. He's good people. And he's rich enough not to care what anybody thinks,' she continued. 'Owns a supermarket,' she said by way of explanation.

They spoke for fifteen minutes, then Jenna left to speak with some friends, and Zaky felt cheerful enough to listen more closely to another admirer named Kenya, and he soon became engrossed in an erotic conversation that left both of them breathless, sweaty, and impatient for the yacht to return to shore.

The yacht docked just after sunset. But Zaky went home alone, because Kenya had drunk herself into incoherent limpness.

Later that night, as Zaky paced his room trying to think of some activity to distract him from his disappointment over Kenya, he heard the sound of a car crunching the gravel in his driveway. He went outside to the balcony, and Jenna waved to him from the passenger window of her boyfriend's Mercedes.

'Can we come in?' she called.

'Of course,' Zaky answered.

'This is Rush,' she said as they came onto the balcony. 'Rush, Zaky.'

115

The men shook hands.

'Nice view,' Rush said.

'Yes,' Zaky agreed. 'I can sit here for hours just looking at the sea. Care for a drink?'

'Rum and Coke for me,' Jenna said. 'Rush can't stay.'

Rush shrugged resignedly. 'That's me: rush, rush, rush!' he said and laughed with loud approval at his joke.

After they had seen Rush to his car, Zaky took Jenna's hand. 'He's okay,' he said.

'Uh-huh,' Jenna agreed.

'Why didn't you drive?' Zaky asked.

'A single woman, driving alone to visit a single man? What would people say?' she asked.

'How long can you stay?' he asked.

'How long do you want?' she replied.

'I must warn you I'm in a mood for bad things,' he said.

'I thought so. That's why I came. Always ready to help,' she said.

For a second, Zaky remembered Anemony's face, and a pang of guilt and loneliness rushed across his face.

'What's wrong?' Jenna asked.

'This is too good to be true. I'm waiting for the bad news,' he replied.

'We're grown-ups,' Jenna said, and went into the kitchen to make herself a drink.

Zaky took Jenna home at midnight. She left him sated, drained, but confused. When he returned home, he was overcome with longing for Anemony. The next day, he asked the secretary to hold all his telephone calls. Jenna would expect him to call as soon as he came in, and she would call when he did not. He did not want to talk to her before he wrote to Anemony.

He wrote three pages, telling her he had settled comfortably, had a good job, and was miserable without her. He invited her to visit – at his expense. And he asked her to marry him – he was sure that she would like his family and his country. He left the office to post the letter himself. When he returned, there were five messages for him; three from Jenna.

'Where were you?' she asked anxiously when he called.

'You left me too tired to talk,' he joked, trying to think of some way to end the call. He longed for an hour of quiet reflection so that he could let his anguish leak slowly out of his mind.

'C'mon, I've been worried. Is it me?' she asked.

'No, Jenna. I was caught at the post office. Thanks for visiting me last night . . . and staying. That was a beautiful thing to do. Now, you're stuck with me . . . because I'm not going to let you get away. You're a jewel of great price.'

'You bullshitter,' Jenna laughed, 'but don't stop. As long as it's nice bullshit.'

'When can I see you again?' Zaky asked, and before she could answer, he added quickly, 'But not tonight, I'm exhausted.'

'Same here,' she said, 'and sore . . . I'll be in touch. But keep the weekend open for me, sweetheart. Now, gotta go.'

'You can have all the weekends you want. See you,' he replied, and hung up.

Anemony's letter arrived four weeks later. Zaky tore the note inside in his anxiety to open the envelope. He glanced quickly at the bottom of the letter to see whether she signed off with 'love'. Satisfied, he read slowly, his eyes brimming as he heard her voice speaking the words:

> *Dear Zaks,*
>
> *You old bastard, thought you'd never write. It was super hearing from you, at long last! The night you left, I cried and cried something fierce. Didn't think I was going to miss you so much. Every now and then, I still do, especially on Friday nights. Wish I had your address when you left, wanted to ask you to cut IT off and send it to me! I miss that too! (laugh).*
>
> *Enjoying your weather? We've had a couple of good days. The bloody sun actually shone for three days, thought it was a miracle. Kids went crazy. Nice though.*
>
> *I met a chap a couple weeks ago. He comes from your island, but says he doesn't know you. Thought all of you islanders knew each other! I went out with him because I wanted to have something I could connect with you. He's pretty good with the kids. Takes them to the park and the cinema. Even the boy's quiet with him. Don't know what's going to happen, but he may be good for me.*
>
> *Now why did you go and ask me to marry you? It almost killed me when you left. I think you liked me, but I loved you something awful. Now you're gone and so far*

*away. And how would you manage with two kids, and one
with a serious problem? It wouldn't work, love. You're too
irresistible. I'd be fighting all day to keep you. I'll marry
your memory. That I can hold on to forever. Someday,
when I stop crying over you, I'll give my bloke a chance. He
may even make a lady out of me.*

> *Got to go now love. Write soon,*
> *Love and kisses (and whatever more you'd like!)*
> *Anemony.*

Zaky reread Anemony's letter four times before he folded it
carefully and put it into a small fireproof safe. Then he turned
the lights out and went to sit on the balcony and stare at the
sea. He prayed that Jenna would not come, or call. At that
moment, he hated her for presuming to take Anemony's place.
And he hated Anemony's new boyfriend – the son of a bitch,
getting to his woman by pretending to love children. He hated
Anemony too – because she was right.

The following Friday, he decided to spend the weekend with
his family.

'Want me to come with you?' Jenna asked.

'Not this time. Too many family things to get straight,' he
replied. On the way home, he stopped at Rush's *FoodWorld* to
buy whiskey for his brothers, a can of assorted biscuits for his
mother, and several pounds of sweets and imported apples and
grapes, for his nephews and nieces.

He arrived at Mahôt at lunchtime, giving Ma Charlotte the
joy of complaining about his unannounced arrival, and of
hurrying to cook more food than Zaky could look at.

When he had eaten enough to ensure his immobility for an
hour or two, his mother began at the top of her list of complaints.
'You don't even call. We don't even know what is happening
with you. Your old friend, the dance teacher, is always asking
about you. Mr. Stephen has to come *here* to ask how you are.
But what is happening with you, Zaky? Must be some woman
doing that to you. I know these young woman in the capital.
Look nice . . . but wait! As soon as they have you, they make you
forget your family and your friends. I bet you don't go to church.
Eh?' She paused for breath. 'When was the last time you went
to church?' she continued, sensing that she had him cornered.

'Give me a break, Ma,' Zaky pleaded. 'I know how you all feel, but I'm trying to get settled again. This is like being in a strange country. I keep remembering things how they were and ... I don't know. I am going to help the boys with the copra this afternoon. If you want, I'll go to church with you tomorrow.' He did not think it prudent to mention Jenna.

'We'll see,' Ma Charlotte said, 'but I don't like what you've been doing. You hear?'

'Yes, Ma,' Zaky replied.

Later, when he was better able to carry the weight of his burdened stomach, Zaky drove to the family farm with his gifts. The old gravel and turf road seemed exactly as it had done the last time Zaky travelled along it; he even believed he could recognize the same *vetiver* and *lantana* bushes that bordered the road; and the old 'throne' was still there – four rocks that lay together in a chair-like arrangement. As a child, Zaky would sit on his jagged 'throne' dispensing laws and justice to the guava, soursop, and sugar-apple subjects that nodded obediently before him.

The city was beginning to fade here, and he could remember Jenna's voice but not her face. He wished he had worn clothes that could find companionship with the dirt and the smoke-stained timbers of the copra house.

Matthew heard the sound of the car and came out to meet him. Zaky got out of the car; and the smell of smoke, cooking and dry leaves rushed at him like old friends who thought they had been forgotten and couldn't wait to remind him of all the things they had enjoyed together.

'Eh! It's you!' Matthew called.

'How are you?' Zaky replied.

'Who is it?' Mark's voice called from the rubble-walled building.

'It's me. Zaky!' Zaky shouted.

Mark and John came out of the small door, brightening the day even further with grins that stretched their faces until their cheeks hurt.

'Where's Luke?' Zaky asked.

'Gone to get water,' Mark replied.

'So how are you?' each one asked, wanting to know for himself.

'So how is Cyrina? And Marcelle? And Julie? And the children?' Zaky asked, to complete the courtesies.

Then it became the turn of the workers to ask about him. How was England? Did he see the Queen? And the Duke! And the Tower of London? And the River Thames? Eh-eh! All the things in the schoolbooks! Aaaaah! They did not forget to reproach him too, but mildly. 'You should come and spend more time with us. Come and eat some good food. Come and enjoy some fresh country air.'

'So you're going to stay and help us?'

'What d'you want me to do?' Zaky asked.

And the workers roared with laughter. 'You're going to put these soft hands on the coconuts? Ah! you must be crazy. And in your nice clothes! Just sit down and relax, man.'

Zaky smiled and shook his head. 'Not joking. I bet I can shell copra as fast as anybody here.'

'Uh-huh,' they said.

He sat on a small bench near a pile of split coconuts from which the fibrous husks had been removed and which had been baked to drive off the moisture from the flesh. A young woman sitting on a bench nearby handed him a short, blunt knife, and waited to see him use it. The desiccated flesh came off easily, but when he tried to match the speed of the others, his hands soon became raw and he cut his left thumb twice against the sharp edges of the shells. But Zaky persisted, because he could not tear his eyes away from the full breasts of the woman who had handed him the knife. She was not wearing a brassiere, and each time she turned to throw pieces of copra into the pile between them, he could see into her partly opened shirt. When she caught him staring, she smiled without reproach, and continued with her work. At that moment, Zaky wished he had never left Mahôt, never even gone to the capital. Now it was too late; if he came back, they would all see him as a failure and a disgrace to the village. Even the woman sitting across from him, whose hands were too calloused to hold a pen, would not think him man enough to roll on her straw mattress.

Luke returned, and after the greetings, and the questions, and the replies, Zaky went to the car for the gifts he had brought. Some of the children's sweets had to be shared with the workers. Zaky wanted to give something special to the woman whose smile had invited him to look at her breasts. But he realized it would discomfit her. Next time.

Ma Charlotte made Zaky drive her to Mass next morning. She insisted on sitting in a front pew, so that she could allow the congregation generous views of her famous, handsome, and perhaps rich son. After Mass, she insisted that Zaky repeat some of his experiences of London and compare the sights of that city with those of Paris, which the priest had left thirty-five years before. On the way home, she smiled contentedly and said, 'The next time, you must go to communion.'

'Yes, Ma,' Zaky replied judiciously.

On the way home, he stopped to see his dance teacher. She did not let go of his hand for most of the hour he spent with her, and only allowed him to enter his car after he promised to dance with the group at the next village festival.

The calm of the country remained with Zaky for several days. The following Sunday, he drove to Stephen's home, rehearsing his apologies for not calling before. No one came out to the sound of his car, or answered the knock on the door. As he turned away, a slurred voice asked, 'Who's it?'

'Mr. Stephen. It's Zaky,' he answered.

'Zaky?' Stephen called back.

'Yes! Yes! Zaky Christophe!' he shouted back.

'Oh,' Stephen replied uncertainly, 'come in. Door's open.'

Stephen paused, wondering whether he should make some excuse himself and leave – and never come back. He decided to go in, and pushed open the door which hung only from its top hinge. The bottom scraped along the semi-circular groove it had worn into the floor. The room he entered was furnished only with a table and two chairs, and the floorboards under the table were covered with termite droppings. Everything smelled of rot and abandonment. Even the moulds growing on the windowsills looked unhealthy.

Stephen came out of his darkened bedroom. 'So, you've come to see me before I die?' he said.

'I'm sorry,' Zaky replied, 'I should have come earlier. And it's my fault. I didn't know coming back was going to be so difficult.'

He was devastated by the old man's appearance. Stephen obviously had not bathed or shaved for several days, and his clothes carried the smells to prove it. He staggered to one of the chairs, and Zaky forced back his urge to gag from the stink when Stephen spoke again. 'Cheap rum. Last night,' he explained.

121

'Um-hm,' Zaky agreed, hesitant to open his mouth.

'So, tell me what they have you doing,' Stephen said.

'Well, I've been travelling around the country organizing cultural groups, encouraging them to apply for small grants to buy instruments and costumes. I'm cataloguing historical sites and evaluating their usefulness in the tourist industry. You know ... letting visitors see something other than the beach and nightclubs. Some other places are going in for ecotourism: showing the real country.'

'I see,' Stephen said. 'Interesting. They must be rich enough now.'

'Who?' Zaky asked.

'*Who?*' Stephen almost shouted. 'The bastards who are selling their country to every Tom, Dick and Harry from abroad. I'll tell you who: the bastards driving around in these monstrous cars, classifying hillsides as marshes so they can buy the land cheap, then resell it as prime residential property.' He paused to get his breath and to wipe saliva from the corner of his mouth. 'Do you know how many semi-literate millionaires we have. Millionaires on government salaries! Oh Christ, man! You haven't seen what's going on?'

'I don't know ... I'm just finding may way around. I hear things but most of it seems like gossip. I . . . .'

'Listen to me, boy. If you want, you can get rich too. Buy whiskey for the right people. Screw around with the right women. Join the party. Become a representative for your district. Promise the usual shit: rapid industrial and economic growth, development of rural areas. Tell them that you can renegotiate better trade deals with the Europeans or the Americans. They'll believe you, too. A fresh face. A handsome face. Don't worry about the scandals. It will show that you're a man. Get a couple of girls pregnant, too. Family man. Lord Almighty, how could we have let them do this to our country?'

Zaky stood in open-mouthed amazement, shaken by the changes in his old friend and mentor. 'I didn't think it was that bad,' he said uncertainly.

Stephen shook his head sadly. 'It's worse. And I think it's too late to change. Good people – the ones who could change things will not expose their names and families to the nastiness of our politics. Of course, one can always sue for defamation of character – if one could find a judge who wouldn't laugh in one's face. There are still some people who are still old-fashioned enough to be honest. But they're tired. They're giving up.'

'So what . . . what can I do?' Zaky asked.

'Go back, Zaky,' Stephen said. 'Go back to your people. Get out of the city. I would tell you to leave the country, too. But if people like you leave, the country will lose what's left of its soul.'

'I can't do that, Mr. Stephen,' he explained. 'I have a contract . . . a three-year contract.'

'Yes, I know. Well, just be careful. Remember, somebody already has some use for you,' he warned.

Zaky moved to sit, silenced and confused by his friend's outburst. He took a deep breath, unable to find the right words.

Suddenly, Stephen smiled. 'You know, it's been long time since we had time to talk. And look at me: carrying on like that. How is Ma Charlotte, and your brothers? They're well?'

Zaky left after an hour – so depressed that he considered taking Stephen's advice and leaving the city for Mahôt. But the contract remained.

Soon after he arrived home, the telephone rang – as he had expected. He lifted the handset and said, 'Hi! Jenna?'

'Hi,' Jenna answered. 'How did you know it was me?'

'Lucky guess,' Zaky laughed.

'Can I come over?' she asked.

'You'd better,' Zaky replied, feeling in need of a powerful distraction from the memory of his visit to Stephen.

'What's wrong with you?' Jenna asked when she arrived. 'You look sick.'

'Well, I had a . . . not very good afternoon,' he said, and went on to tell her of Stephen's comments.

Jenna listened sympathetically, then shrugged. 'Listen to me, Zaky. Humphrey Stephen is a bitter, resentful old man who'd be doing the same damn thing he's complaining about if he could have kept his mouth out of a whiskey bottle. Now, he wants to complain! You have a good job. You have everything open for you. You'd better stay away from that old man. Who the hell cares about what Humphrey Stephen says?'

He did not feel like any intimacy that night, but Jenna's lotion-softened hands surmounted those emotional impediments.

Before they fell asleep, he turned to her and whispered, 'Jenna? You're fantastic, you know.'

She pushed herself more closely into the curve of his body.

That had not been what he wanted to say. He wanted to say something more romantic; that he wished she could move in with him; or perhaps just simply that he liked her. But he put away those words for the time when he had stopped longing for her to say and do the things Anemony had said and done in bed.

*Chapter 17*

# The price of a favour

Jenna telephoned to say that she was coming to his office to bring him an invitation. 'Can't let this get lost in the mail,' she said, 'and I want some sugar.'

The invitation was for cocktails at the minister's home. 'You'd better come,' she said, laughing; but Zaky did not miss the cautionary tone.

The minister himself greeted them at the door. 'Ah, Jenna,' he said, kissing her on the cheek, 'when I die, I hope to go where all the women look like you.'

'What a nice thing to say, Sir,' Jenna laughed.

'And Mr. Christophe. I hear the government made a wise investment in you,' the minister said, taking Zaky's hand in both of his.

'Thank you very much, Sir,' Zaky answered.

Inside, he said to Jenna, 'I didn't know that the guy knew me.'

'Come on, Zaky, you should know that everybody in the city knows everything that goes on. Everything.' And she glanced knowingly at him.

Zaky looked at the swirl of jewellery and tailored clothes around him, and wondered what he had ever loved about the hills and villages of Rocher. He smiled at the thought of himself on the family estate: listening to his brothers argue about forcing more copra in to a jute-fibre bag. He would be given the task of holding the bag open, while one of the workers used a tall wooden pestle to force more dried coconut into the bag: a heavy pole, polished with coconut oil, pounding one more penny into the bag, 'Hunh ... hunh!' He imagined himself growing old under the coconut and banana trees, lusting after country girls too strong and swift to stay in his hold.

He was more comfortable breathing French perfumes; wearing comfortable wool and silk; and pretending not to notice the eyes inviting seduction.

Later in the evening, the minister walked over. 'Listen, Zaky, I want to talk to you next week. My secretary will call you. Okay? Now enjoy yourself, and keep an eye on Miss Marais. That is some woman!'

'Yes Sir,' Zaky replied, flattered.

Jenna was standing with a group that had stayed together for most of the evening. After the introductions, Zaky wondered why the men and women smiling and talking to him all seemed familiar. It was on his return with drinks for himself and Jenna that he remembered Humphrey Stephen sitting at his crumbling table, drunk and filthy, shouting, '... bastards ... millionaires on government salaries ....' The laughing and joking continued, and Zaky joined in, comfortable with them ... comfortable with their success.

In the following months, his new friends demonstrated their trust and confidence by soliciting small loans from him. In return, he was able to get electronic equipment through customs without tariffs; or buy liquor at greatly reduced prices. Occasionally, the wife of a friend would visit his home to ask, between tears, for advice about her husband's suspected infidelities, or her own financial straits. And she would leave comforted by his body or his dollars after an hour in his bedroom.

It was almost one year later, that the minister himself called to invite Zaky to meet him at his own convenience. They met two hours later. The minister's secretary ushered him into a room whose walls were hung with paintings by local artists; and spread around the office were tall wooden carvings of abstract subjects, also by local sculptors. There were no imported art pieces. The minister noticed Zaky's interest. 'Got to support our own,' the minister said.

'It's very impressive, Sir,' Zaky replied.

'Well, how's the job?' the minister asked.

'I'm enjoying it, Sir,' Zaky replied.

'Good, good. And Jenna Marais? Taking care of you?'

'Sir?' Zaky said, his face burning with embarrassment.

The minister laughed. 'Didn't mean to fluster you. That woman makes a man hate old age. Now let's talk ...'

The minister pointed to a small table with two chairs in one corner of the office. He sat with his fingers steepled in over-powering supplication to his guest. 'Now my friend, I want your advice on an important matter. Termites!'

'Termites, Sir?' Zaky asked, looking around for evidence of insect devastation.

'Yessir, Mr. Christophe. Termites! The greatest threat to wooden structures is termites! Now what if you could provide timber that was resistant to termites? Strong, beautiful, fragrant timber?' the minister continued.

'Make good money, Sir,' Zaky answered.

'Yes! Zacharias Christophe. Yes!' The minister shouted as if he had just been granted a vision of heaven. 'Now listen to this. A couple years ago, we had a proposal from a group of investors who wanted to put several million dollars into a project at Rocher ... your area. They wanted to harvest the *laurier canelles* trees in the forests on Manuage, especially around Tambour. They'd put in roads ... schools ... other things. The representative for Rocher mentioned it quietly to a couple of folks there, but people didn't seem too interested. Especially the people of Tambour ... they chased him off and threatened to "cut off his balls" if he came back.' The minister stopped and chuckled. 'If he had any balls in the first place, he wouldn't have run away. Well anyway, I can't let a group of farmers impede the development of the country. And they'll get most of the benefit anyway. I can't see why they're so adamant about walking around barefoot and poor. I came from the country myself. Like you, I know how hard life is out there. We need you to help us on this one, Zaky. And you won't regret it.' He stopped and stared unblinkingly at Zaky. 'So, what do you think?'

'You've caught me by surprise, Sir. I'll need to think about this ... how I go about this ... for a while. I'll get working on it. I think I can talk to the people of Tambour. When do you want me to get back to you, Sir?' he asked.

'Take your time, Zaky,' the minister said. 'We don't want any trouble in those hills. These people don't play around. And we don't want them chasing after financiers with machetes. And us too! So, I'll be hearing from your. But don't take too long. Eh?'

The minister escorted Zaky to the hallway outside his office, with his arms around the younger man's shoulders. The staff looked at Zaky with intense interest, trying to read the purpose of the meeting from his eyes and face.

The next evening, Zaky drove immediately to Humphrey Stephen's home. This time, Stephen was sober and relatively clean; his beard was only three days old. The reception was friendlier, if a little wary. 'How are you, Mr. Stephen?' Zaky greeted him.

'A big shot like you, still calling me 'Mr.' Don't get that kind of respect much now. But I'm fine. How's Ma Charlotte and your brothers?'

'Everybody's fine,' Zaky answered.

'So, what brings you over here?' Stephen asked.

'I need some advice. Yesterday, I had a meeting with the minister. These guys are planning to harvest timber from the forests on Manuage. I checked the plans, they will have to cut a road right through the middle of Tambour. Some houses on Latanier will have to be moved. But . . . the people of Mahôt and Amande will benefit because the road would shorten the distance to the town of Rocher. Anyway, if they damage the rainforests on the steep hillsides, rains are going to wash away all the soil. A lot of people are going to lose their farms. And their water. Oh shit, man!' Zaky said, his face ashen.

Stephen leaned forward. 'See how they make sure you get something out of it? Oh yes. They will take care of their friends. What are you going to do?'

'I'm going to talk to my family; and then I'm going to Tambour to talk to the people there again. The representative for Rocher spoke to them about it, but . . . .'

'But they ran him off!' Stephen laughed out loudly. 'I heard he arrived in town covered in mud . . . and cursing, saying that they should put a wall around Tambour . . . the damn place was a zoo . . . savage animals. Wish I'd been there.'

'Oh God, what am I going to do?' Zaky moaned.

'When I had my choices, I made the wrong one. Don't do like me, Zaky. Look around you. Look at this valley behind you. When you go back to Rocher, go up to Tambour, go up to the pasture above the village . . . where Mabouya goes to sit. Look around. Look at the hills and the sea. This is the most beautiful place in the world. No one who has climbed to the top of these hills and looked around has not wanted to cry with regret at having to climb down again. Ask anyone born on this small island – who has lived in New York, or London, or Toronto all his life – where he comes from. And he will tell you it is here! Here! Zaky. Not Canada or England or America. Please, man, don't touch these hills. They aren't yours . . . or any government's.'

For several minutes, they were both silent. Stephen brushed his sleeve against his nose; and Zaky looked away, afraid that his friend was crying.

Finally, Zaky spoke to Stephen. 'I still must discuss it with the people at Tambour . . . even if I don't agree with the plan. If I don't do it, they will send somebody else. I want you to come with me.'

'Yes, I'll come with you. And you must talk to Mabouya. There are things you should know,' Stephen replied.

'How about next Sunday?' Zaky suggested.

'Well, you can see how busy I am,' Stephen said, smiling sadly.

'Okay then, next Saturday morning, about six. I'll 'phone my mother to say we're coming. Got to go now.'

'Good to see you again, Zaky,' Stephen called out, as the car moved away.

Jenna wanted to go with them to Rocher, but Zaky thought it impolitic to have her and Stephen so close together, and he wanted to discuss strategy with Stephen.

Along the way, they stopped for a drink at a roadside bar outside one of the small, fishing villages that hugged the coastal road. The two old customers sitting inside playing dominoes and the lady behind the bar recognized Stephen as he came in. 'Eh! Mr. Stephen. We haven't seen you for so long,' the lady said. 'And who is the nice man with you?' She looked at Zaky. 'Mr. Nice Man, come in . . . come in. Um-um-um! If I was only twenty years younger. But I have two nice daughters . . . .'

'Ma Alix!' Stephen called out. 'Behave yourself! This is Mr. Christophe. He is a big shot with the government. We're going to Rocher.'

'I hope he's not going to ask them to put any hotel there,' one of the men said.

Before Stephen or Zaky could answer, the other man said, 'Christophe . . . Christophe? Eh! You're Edouard's son?'

'Yes,' Zaky replied.

'You were abroad?'

'Yes, in England.'

'Ah! I knew your father well. My mother came from Tambour. Got an old Carib drummer there. She said he was an old man when she was a child.'

'Must be somebody else. Mabouya couldn't be that old,' his companion said.

'You know Mabouya, Mr. Stephen? How old you think he is?' asked the first man.

Stephen shrugged. 'I'm not going to ask him,' he said, and turned to the lady. 'I'll have a Coke.' He looked at Zaky. 'You . . .?'

'Beer,' Zaky answered.

The two other customers turned back to their game. 'So, you're telling me the man is over one hundred years old?' one asked.

The other slammed a tile into place on the table. 'Ah! I see! They got a bunch of Caribs, all named Mabouya, playing drums at Tambour for over a hundred years. Eh, asshole?' he enquired.

His adversary countered his move with another tile; the other followed. Slap! Slap! Slap! Each blow ground a little further into the table top, while the two old players interspersed their taunts and insults with deafening reaffirmations of their friendship.

Zaky sipped his beer and smiled towards the two men, who were engrossed again in their game. He turned his gaze to the woman; she beamed back at him in a way that suggested she was already planning her daughter's wedding feast. They finished their drinks and left the bar to calls of 'Walk well' that were almost drowned out by the clattering of tiles.

Zaky drove in self-absorbed silence for several minutes before glancing at Stephen.

'What was that about Mabouya?' he asked, repeating the question when Stephen did not answer.

Finally, Stephen asked, 'You believe in ghosts?'

'When I was a kid, I think I did. Why? You're going to tell me Mabouya's a ghost?' Zaky laughed.

Stephen continued, 'Some years ago, the parish priest at Rocher asked me to have a look at some old documents he had found in the church records. They were notes made by a French priest about two hundred years ago. Name was L'Abbé Joubert. Well, there was mention of a fantastic drum with terrifying powers that he had seen in a village on Manuage. There were sketches and descriptions of the drum. There was also an account of the owner of the drum. An old Carib named Mabouya.'

'What?' Zaky shouted. 'What are you saying? Mabouya is over two hundred years old?'

'That's exactly what I said,' Stephen replied. 'So one day ... the last time you and I went there together ... I asked him about it. Wouldn't answer then, but on another occasion, he asked me to climb the hill with him, to that little pasture up there. Told me the history of Manuage and Tambour and Rocher. Knows the ancestor of everybody on the hills. Says you are the sixth generation of Christophes. Says you're descended from an African named François.

Zaky had pulled to a stop on the shoulder of the road. He stared hard at Stephen. 'Holy shit! Holy shit!' was all he was able to say.

'You're right,' said Stephen, 'and crazy shit too.'

'Told anyone else? Zaky asked.

Stephen shook his head.

'But where did the drum come from? It has African animals on it,' Zaky said.

'His teacher was another escaped slave the Caribs called Entahso ... they couldn't pronounce his real name properly. Mabouya was to safeguard the drum until he found a suitable apprentice. Just as he had been. But no family would give up a child to be apprenticed to a strange old man. So Mabouya continues. Continues ... continues.'

Zaky gripped Stephen's arm so strongly that the older man pulled away in alarm.

'Mr. Stephen! Mr. Stephen!' Zaky cried. 'You won't believe this, but when I was about five, I started having these dreams.

131

About an old man taking away a drum my father had just given me. The dreams went on for years. Until I went to England. That's why I have always wanted to beat that drum. That's *my* drum!'

Stephen took a deep breath, but did not say any more. They did not find much worth saying the rest of the way.

The travellers arrived at Mahôt one hour later. Stephen's revelations had left Zaky in a state of nervous agitation, and he was trying to fashion some excuse to explain his loss of appetite. Then the smells of his mother's cooking embraced him outside her open door. As usual, Ma Charlotte had overburdened her lunch table. Soon, Stephen was shovelling his mother's food, gnawing fragments of meat from the bones, and pursuing errant grains of rice. The look of pleasure on his mother's face as she urged them on quieted the turbulence in his head. When Zaky and Stephen pleaded that they could eat no more, she went into the kitchen and returned with a plate of fried plantains dusted with sugar. The men discovered they could eat some more. Zaky hoped the people of Tambour had eaten well too.

## Chapter 18

# Return of the first ones

Zaky noticed at once that the orchids on the hillsides near Tambour were not as abundant as at their last visit. Stephen sensed his thoughts. 'Damn tourists,' he said. 'Can't take the orchids past Customs, but they still pull them up. Plants can't live anywhere else. And they won't listen. Should break a couple of damn arms.'

Zaky did not answer; he was looking for the *Epidendrum nocturnum*. He thought he saw two plants with single white flowers on an inaccessible ledge on a cliff face. Stephen followed his glance and swore. 'See? Only two plants left. Good thing they had the sense to grow up there,' he said angrily.

Minutes after Zaky parked his car at the bottom of the path that led uphill to Tambour, word of his arrival with Humphrey Stephen leaped from house to house in the village.

'Eh! Zaky. Eh! M'sieu Stephen . . . .' the villagers greeted the visitors, and then followed them to Janvier Sivien's small shop – the accepted place for meetings. The greetings were short this time, because the visitors' faces showed the seriousness of the things they had come to say. 'So, my friend Zaky,' Sivien said, 'I hear the government has big plans for us. A couple of years ago, we told them the plans were too big.' Sivien paused to acknowledge the scattered laughter.

Zaky laughed. 'Yes,' he said, 'this time they sent someone whose balls come from here. I heard what you did.'

Even Mabouya laughed this time; it had been so long since he had witnessed a good rout.

'People of Tambour,' Zaky said. 'I won't lie to you. The government sent me here to ask you to cooperate with them to develop the economy of the area. My job is to tell you what they promise you will get from the project they have in mind.

133

You will have to make up your minds about it. I can tell you that. Since the government pays my salary, I have to give their point of view.

'The plan is to build a timber-processing plant up there – above Tambour. There is a lot of good, old *laurier canelle* trees around here. That wood is very, very valuable, and there will always be a good market for it. There will be good jobs for many people here. You know where the trees are, and tractors will not be able to get to all the mature trees. Many will have to be cut by hand. You can do that. The government will compensate you for the loss of your property; and you will have to rebuild the village lower down the hill. What else will you get from the development? Well, a better road to Rocher, a good market right here for your produce, and jobs for the younger people . . . a lot of jobs.'

There was silence for some minutes. 'We will have to discuss these things,' the old villager named Charlo said. 'This is going to take time.'

Sivien, whom the other villagers called No-no because a nervous tick made him shake his head continually – as if in interdiction of voices in his head clamouring to be heard – spoke up. 'Messieurs, dames,' he began, shaking his head vigorously at the ground. 'I know what I will say, and I will tell you now, my answer is no. No-no-no! I don't want my children and grandchildren carrying wood for other people. Tambour people should not be servants. And one thing you didn't tell us: when we cut down the forest, the rain will wash the soil away. We will lose our land. And maybe our lives. There will be landslides.'

The other voices joined in. Vivienne, Charlo's wife, coughed to get their attention. 'The government wants to know what we think, Mr. Zaky. Or are they telling us what they plan to do when they're ready?'

'Ah, Ma Charlo,' Zaky answered, 'I wish I could answer that without having to think about it. The problem is, if you say no to this, how are you going to ask for something you will need in the future: like piped water, a school, a post office?'

'We have been here a long time without these things. We have managed,' several voices said.

'Well, think about it carefully,' Zaky warned.

'Tell us, Mr. Zaky, what you think,' a woman asked.

'No,' Zaky answered. 'That won't be fair.'

'Mr. Stephen,' another voice called. 'What about you?'

'I shouldn't get into your business,' Stephen answered, 'but I wonder how much somebody is being paid to keep pushing for harvesting timber up there. These trees are hundreds of years old. Who will replace them? You know how I feel anyway. I don't like it. Not on Manuage. You can harvest the trees yourselves. One tree at a time, giving the forest time to recover.'

'Zaky,' Sivien said, 'let us go home and think about this. Stay here tonight. You can leave tomorrow.'

Zaky looked at Stephen. The latter nodded; he would be more comfortable here that at his own home.

As the meeting broke up, Zaky walked up to Mabouya and took him by the elbow. 'M'sieu Mbouya,' he said, 'if you have a little time, you think I could walk up the hill with you? Mr. Stephen told me I should look at the hills from the pasture above the village.'

Mabouya thought for a moment, then said, 'Look at me, Christophe's son, you're not going to make my life miserable over that drum again, eh?'

'Not today, M'sieu Mabouya, but another day we'll talk about that again,' Zaky promised, laughing.

Stephen went with Sivien to continue the rare opportunities for feasting that this day had brought. Others watched with curiosity as Zaky and Mabouya walked along the road that led uphill from the village, but that curiosity was not enough to persuade anyone to follow ... not after Mabouya.

Mabouya sat on the large rock that his pants had kept free from lichens and moss. Zaky sat nearby on a patch of grass free from the thorny mimosas.

'Mr. Stephen told me about the history of Manuage,' Zaky said. 'About you and the slaves who came here to escape from the plantations. He said you knew my ancestors. But why haven't you told these things to anybody, M'sieu Mabouya?'

Mabouya turned slowly towards Zaky. 'An old Carib comes to you and says he is over two hundred years old, that he was one of the first people here, that he learned the drum from a master drummer from Africa; and you're going to believe that? You're going to leave me alone to beat my drum at your festivals? Eh?'

135

'But someday, somebody would want to find out how come their grandparents knew you when you were old. I myself heard a man mention this on my way here. No, M'sieu Mabouya, you could not go on like that.'

'That is why I wanted an apprentice drummer. It is time for me to go back to my own people.'

'Your own people? Where?'

'Over there.' Mabouya pointed west, towards the horizon. 'My people came from there. Somebody is waiting for me.'

'Waiting for you? But it is over two hundred years . . .'

'Yes, I know, but the voice is still calling. I can hear it asking for me . . . when the wind blows strong up the hill.'

Zaky frowned, unable to make sense of the old man's words.

'You see the *imortelle* trees down there?' Mabouya pointed to a grove of trees with blazing red flowers where the path from Tambour met the main road. 'Well, that is where the old leaders of Tambour are buried. François, your ancestor; Entahso, my teacher; Maimouna, François's wife; and Sivien's ancestor is there too. If the government cuts a road to Tambour, they will dig up the old people's bones and throw them away. That is all I have to say.'

The next morning, the people of Tambour came to Sivien's shop again. Sivien spoke for them, his head shaking in contradiction of his words. 'Mr. Christophe. I do not want this thing here. This is my position. But there are many others who disagree. They say we cannot hide here forever from modern times. So, we could not make a decision that everybody wanted. What we are going to tell you is this. We have know you and your father Edouard Christophe, your mother Charlotte, your brothers and their families, all our lives. We are going to ask you to do what you think is best for all of us . . . for you too. Go and tell the government the decision you come to. This is what we think.'

For several minutes, Zaky looked at Sivien's face and at the grey-ringed eyes brimming with painful acceptance, and then he nodded. He said his long goodbyes and he and Stephen drove back in silence to Rocher. In a couple of years, Zaky thought, there would be a broad tarmac road here, making it easier for others to enjoy the incredible, secret beauty of Manuage and its sister hills. The best of the most beautiful country in the world. And he, Zaky Christophe, would have made the decision.

136

There was only time to say goodbye to his family and to let them load the back of his car with more fruit and vegetables than he could eat, and would have to give away when he got to the city.

The two men tried occasionally to make conversation during the long ride back, but only succeeded in making themselves uncomfortable. When they arrived in the city, Stephen asked to be dropped off at the bus depot, pleading that it was too much for Zaky to drive him home and back again. As Zaky drove away from the depot, he looked into the rearview mirror and could see Stephen still standing where he had let him off, looking back at him.

The next morning, he called the minister's office.

'Ah yes, my friend. How did it go?' the minister greeted him.

'I have a decision for you, Sir. The . . .' he began.

'Wait. Not over the 'phone. Come over to my office,' the minister said.

'Ah, Mr. Christophe, Sir,' the minister said when Zaky arrived. When they were seated at the small table where they had spoken before, he leaned forward and spoke. 'Let's hear the good news.'

'The people of Tambour couldn't come to a majority decision,' Zaky answered, 'and they asked that I speak on their behalf.'

The minister frowned. 'That's unusual,' he said. 'So what did you decide?'

'To say no, Sir,' Zaky answered.

The minister's frown deepened as if trying to understand what 'no' meant.

'Eh?' he asked.

'No, Sir,' Zaky repeated. 'The project would destroy Tambour, Manuage hill itself, and the quality of life for the people of Rocher.'

The minister shook his head in bafflement. 'You, Zaky Christophe, have decided to block a multimillion development, because of some shitty sentiment about some quality of life?' he exploded. 'You stupid, arrogant, idiot. Get out of my office. And get the hell out of the office you're in! You're fired! And don't tell me any shit about any contract, smartass. We don't have any contract with you. We don't owe you a damn cent. Just get the hell out of my office. You damn fool! And don't think that

137

will stop us. In a few weeks the bulldozers will be at Rocher ... with the police. No damn country people are going to make decisions for the government. And you're finished in this city. Finished! You hear? Finished!'

Zaky shrugged, and let out a deep breath. It was done. He drove slowly to his office, finding it difficult to drive with his knees trembling so violently. He did not know how he was going to break the news to Jenna. Perhaps he should just clear his office and leave the city. He did not think he would be allowed to remain much longer in his apartment. The telephone rang while he was clearing his desk. He did not answer it. A few minutes later, Jenna walked in. 'I heard,' she said.

Zaky nodded. 'Yep,' he said, 'the world's come to an end.'

'Do you know what you just did, Zaky?' Jenna asked. 'You've just messed up your life and a good career. Nobody, nobody is going to want to see you or talk to you. You've messed up big-big time, sweetheart.'

'I know,' Zaky said, then smiled at her. 'Those are my people in Rocher. I have to live with them.'

'What's going to happen to us, now?' Jenna asked.

'I don't know, Jenna. I don't have any quarrel with you, but I have to get out of here,' Zaky answered. 'I am going back home. I have a family ... and a life there. I can't ask you to come with me. That's another world. You wouldn't like it: too quiet, too hard.'

'You ever felt anything for me, Zaky?' Jenna asked.

'Never wanted anyone else,' Zaky said.

'Change your mind, Zaky. Call the man back. Say you've reconsidered. Don't do this to me, Zaky,' Jenna pleaded. 'Look, the party is filled with old men, old dying men who would starve without the money they can steal from the country. We need good young people like you, Zaky. Change your mind, the party will be glad to take you. Your district representative is already too old to handle the next election. You can run for your district. And you'd win. Then you can help change the things you don't like. Don't leave, Zaky. Please, please, baby.'

'It's too late, Jenna. I am not sorry for what I did. I'm sure it's the right thing.'

Jenna wiped her eyes and nose against her sleeve, took a deep breath, and walked out of the office.

When he arrived at his apartment, the telephone was ringing. After the fifth ring, he picked it up in exasperation. 'Look, Jenna, I . . . ' he began.

'Hey, Zaky. It's me, Rush,' the caller said.

'Hi, Rush. How's things?' Zaky replied.

'Rushing ahead,' Rush chuckled. 'Look man, Jenna asked me to call. Wants me to talk sense into your head. Girl's in love with you like you wouldn't believe. Thinks you're a little crazy, though.'

'So, you think I was stupid, too?' Zaky asked.

'Look, Zaky. A few years ago, I had to decide whether I should go on pretending to be something I wasn't . . . I think you know what I'm talking about. Fortunately, I had enough money to keep some of my friends. Anyway, every now and then, it's good to see somebody stand up for something. No, I don't think you were stupid. I didn't call to ask you to change your mind. I called to ask you not to change it. But tell me, man, why are you really doing this?' Rush answered.

'Well, I had actually planned to go ahead with the minister's plan. Then I remembered a girl I went out with in London, and it suddenly hit me that that was the last time I was really truly happy.'

'Gad! She was that beautiful? Or that good?' Rush said.

'Not really. Her life wasn't anything to boast about, but she was satisfied and happy with the little she had. Used to make me feel that she was only interested in making me happy. And I still feel guilty about the little that she got from me. I've never felt that contented with anybody else. I was thinking about her and I know what she would say if I could ask what I should do. Think she'd be proud of me now. But I'm worried about Jenna. You think they'll . . .?

Rush interrupted him. 'No, don't worry. Nobody's going to touch her. She knows too much about too many people. That girl can take care of herself. And if she's in trouble, I'll watch out for her. Well, keep in touch. You can get a discount at *FoodWorld* anytime. See you, and when things settle down, come back for Jenna. Take care, Zaky Christophe,' Rush said.

'You too, Rush'.

His brothers drove a truck to the city to help him move his furniture and belongings. He spent his last night at Jenna's apartment, where they struggled to find the right words to say the things rushing through their minds. They said little until it was time for Zaky to leave; then there were too many things to say. And it was too late now to tell her all the good things he had put aside for a better time.

One month later he was at home, at Mahôt, going over the family's business accounts, when Jenna telephoned. 'Zaky? It's me. Jenna . . .'

'Jenna!' Zaky cried in delight.

'Listen, Zaky,' she spoke quickly, 'can't chat now. They are sending two bulldozers and a van loaded with police to Tambour . . . tomorrow. The police have machine guns. Please take care. I'm afraid, Zaky. Bye.'

'Hello? Hello?' he shouted into the telephone, but she had already hung up.

Ma Charlotte came into the room, alarmed by the shouting. 'What's going on?' she asked.

'The government. Sending tractors to Tambour. Got to get up there,' he answered, and ran to his car before she could speak.

She immediately set out to the farmhouse to alert her other sons.

Later that evening, Humphrey Stephen arrived. 'News all over the city,' he told an agitated Ma Charlotte and her four older sons. 'Where's Zaky?' he asked.

'Gone to Tambour,' Matthew said.

'They told the press to stay away, and they're stopping all traffic coming this way,' Stephen continued. 'I got a ride on a bus to Rocher. Some young man brought me here on the back of his motorcycle . . . through the bush! I will never do that again. Somebody give me a ride to Tambour?'

When Zaky arrived at Tambour, the adults were already waiting at the bottom of the path that led to the village. Old people, used to eliminating disputes with deluges of words, stood ready for battle armed with machetes, stones and clubs. The young men had already removed their shirts, ready to repel all foes with displays of bared chests and corded muscles. They held machetes and Molotov cocktails.

A little later, Zaky's brothers arrived with Stephen. They stayed until dark, and left at Zaky's insistence. Stephen refused to leave. When darkness came, the villagers agreed that it was safe to return to their homes to eat and sleep.

The next morning they reassembled, their tiredness from a sleepless night turning to rage at the people who had kept them away from their gardens and families.

Just before noon, they heard the sound of powerful diesel engines. Soon a black van crowded with police appeared, followed by two fourteen-wheeled tractor-trailers each loaded with an orange bulldozer. The villagers massed at the place where the orchids once grew within reach. The police vehicle stopped two hundred feet away, and a policeman in the khaki uniform of a senior officer approached them. The captain was armed only with a baton because all he wanted from this encounter was a drink of coconut-water, some vegetables for dinner, and a long chat with the old people. His men carried ammunition, but he had ordered them not to load their weapons. 'Ladies and gentlemen, people of Tambour, good afternoon,' he greeted them when he was near enough to see their expressions.

'Good afternoon, M'sieu Policeman,' they answered.

'I think you know why I'm here,' he said. 'The government has sent the tractors to begin clearing a road to the top of the hill. We will not touch the village. That is something you and the government will have to work out. The police were sent to guard the tractors. We are not here to look for trouble. I myself, all I want is to sit down for a while, then go home and be with my family.'

The villagers nodded, silently complimenting the police officer on choosing the right words. Then Sivien spoke. 'We understand you have your job to do. We have ours, too. We have to protect our land and our families. As soon as your tractors cut the ground here, the hill will begin to bleed, and you will begin taking our lives away. We cannot let you do this. Mr. Christophe spoke for us. We do not want any logging here. That is what we have decided. And that is all we have to say, M'sieu Policeman.'

The officer turned towards Zaky. 'Mr. Christophe?' he said.

'I'm sorry, Sir. You will have to use force to do what you were sent to do. These people will not change their minds.'

'And that is your last word?' he asked.

'Yes!' the villagers shouted.

141

'I see,' the officer responded, and turned back to the waiting vehicles. 'Okay,' he told the policemen sweltering in the van, 'disembark. Stand with weapons at the ready. Remember, no shooting. No crap from anybody. I want you to precede the bulldozers. All right; let's get in line.'

The policemen formed a line to face the crowd, and the officer went to supervise the unloading of the bulldozers. The ground shivered as the diesel engines roared into life, and the earthmovers unfolded their war banners of black smoke. The invaders moved forward slowly.

The villagers looked at the rifles, the huge advancing machines, and then looked at Zaky. 'Well, people of Tambour, if you want to change your minds, we can move to let the tractors pass.'

'No!' several voices said.

'You think they'll shoot?' someone asked.

'I don't think so . . . not unless we hurt one of them. Most of these police are country boys. They don't want to kill anybody. I'm with you in this. When the tractor gets here, I'm going to lie down in front of it. There aren't enough police to arrest everybody.'

'But they will arrest you,' Mabouya observed.

Zaky shrugged, and went to sit in the path of the approaching column. Stephen and several other men and women joined him.

The police column stopped. 'Load your weapons,' the captain ordered.

Humphrey Stephen heard the clicks of ammunition magazines locking into place. He rose, 'I'm going to talk to the captain,' he said to Zaky. 'We are not going to have bloodshed here today. My God . . . this has already gone much too far.'

He was twenty feet away when Zaky saw his friend's shirt billow, and saw the old man stagger as if a quick gust of wind had pushed him backwards. Then the report of the rifle crashed against their ears, bounced back from the hillside and rang again and again in their hearing. They saw the body of Humphrey Stephen fold to the ground, writhe, then lie still. A bad dream: a grotesque, deafening, paralyzing nightmare.

'Oh my God!' the captain screamed. 'Who told you to fire? Who fired that shot?'

A young policeman dropped his rifle to the ground. He was trembling violently; his pants soiled with urine and excrement.

142

'He panicked, Sir,' an older policeman said.

Zaky rose. 'Give me a machete,' he said.

Someone passed him the blade. Slowly the villagers advanced towards the police.

The captain's voice shook as he spoke to his men. 'When I give the order, fire above their heads. Do not fire at anybody until I say so. I will shoot anyone who does not follow my orders.'

A few seconds later, he shouted, 'Fire!'

The villagers winced, waiting for the pain of shattered bones and shredded flesh. Then they quickened their pace.

'Lower your rifles,' the captain ordered. 'Ready . . .'

The sound came like a great roar from the ground beneath them. The hills and trees heaved as another immeasurable, overpowering noise flung the people to the ground, wrenching firearms, machetes, stones and clubs from enfeebled hands. Those who had fallen on their backs saw the sky turn the colour of bloody ash. Others with their faces pressed into the ground retched from the stink of putrefaction. The sounds came again, rolling down the hill, breaking against their bodies like avalanches of mud, filling their ears and chests, driving even terror from their minds. They heard the pounding of massive feet blasting into the ground; and the thunder of voices that beat into their chests:

'François!'

'Hai!'

'Entahso!'

'Hai!'

'Sivien!'

'Hai!'

'Ma-bou-ya!'

'Hai!'

All imaginings and sensations flew from the minds of the villagers and police, and they lay like infants on the ground, mewling and whimpering.

Mabouya stopped, his hands resting on the drum skin until they had regained their normal brown colour. Then he set the drum aside to pick his way through the prostrate bodies to where Stephen lay. He squatted near the body and raised Stephen's head. 'It's time for me to go, too,' he said to the still face.

The captain managed to get his men back into the van. He would have to drive back the company of fouled, wet, dazed and trembling men. He collected the guns, and threw them into the back. He drove away with the motor in first gear, because he did not trust his trembling limbs to work the clutch and gears. The bulldozer drivers had fled, leaving the engines idling.

Slowly, carefully, the villagers stood up and began making their way back to Tambour. Zaky and three others carried Stephen's body to his car. Later, when he had regained some coordination, he would drive the body to Rocher.

That night, in the capital, the minister sat in his darkened kitchen waiting for the telephone to ring. It was almost morning when it rang; and when he picked it up, his voice failed and he sighed into the handset.

'We heard of your problem,' scratched a voice, dry and brittle as chalk. 'The project is cancelled. We said no blood. You will remember, of course, that we advanced you thirty thousand dollars.'

'Sir? Sir?' the minister called desperately into the telephone, but all he heard were the chirps and beeps of telecommunication links being broken.

One week later, three mechanics arrived at Tambour in a pickup truck. They unloaded drums of fuel into the bulldozers' tanks, then drove the tractors back on to their transports. It took them an hour to turn the awkward vehicles around; then they headed down the hill.

Mabouya sent word that he wanted to see Zaky. When the latter arrived, they walked up to the small pasture.

'It's time for me to go,' Mabouya said,' and I want you to help me buy a small canoe. I do not have much money.'

Zaky nodded. 'I'll pay for it,' he said. 'What about the drum. Who will beat the drum?' he asked, his throat tight with fear.

'You are now *Maître du Tambour*,' Mabouya answered.

'But I can't beat the drum like you,' Zaky protested.

'I made the drum and took care of it. But it was Entahso's hands that beat it. Make your own drum. Entahso is still here . . . under the *immortelles*.

On the night they had agreed, Zaky drove to Tambour. In the dim light, he saw a shape come from the grove of the tall, ancient trees.

'Turn your lights off and open the trunk ... for the drum,' Mabouya ordered.

Zaky got out to help him. In the light from the car's open trunk, Zaky saw that the Carib was naked and covered in red pigment. 'Will we see you again, M'sieu Mabouya?' Zaky asked.

'No,' Mabouya said.

When they got to the beach, Zaky helped Mabouya load the drum on board the canoe. The only other observer was a mongrel that crawled out from under an overturned canoe. It sat on its haunches watching, and did not move when Zaky kicked some sand at it. The two men pushed the canoe into the water, and Mabouya climbed aboard. He took the single paddle and dug it into the water. 'Carry yourself well, son of Dioub,' he called without looking back.

Zaky watched the canoe disappear into the darkness. He heard the wind pick up, and saw the waves grow heavy.

Mabouya grinned at the swells pushing against his canoe. The water ebbed suddenly, pulling back as if to recall a half-remembered face; then it surged forward, flinging spray in its rush.

# Glossary

| | |
|---|---|
| *acra* | codfish fritter |
| *ajoupa* | a small hut made of thatch |
| *annatto* | an orange-red dye and the plant it comes from |
| *balata* | extremely hard wood |
| *bois bandé* | an aphrodisiac |
| *Coleman lamp* | hurricane lamp |
| *compère* | friend |
| *coulirou* | a jack fish |
| *dachine* | *taro*, a root vegetable |
| *eddoes* | root vegetable |
| *Epidendrum nocturnum* | ground orchid |
| *gens engagé* | a possessed person |
| *gomier* | a tree used in making dugout canoes |
| *imortelle* | a long-lived flowering tree |
| *iouana* | iguana |
| *Ipomoea* | a seaside vine related to morning glory |
| *kurkunu* | Guinea worm |
| *lacomête* | a dance |
| *laurier canelle* | fragrant, termite-resistant wood |
| *macambo* | plantain |
| *macoudja* | passionfruit |
| *Maître de Tambour* | Master Drummer |
| *manicou* | opossum |
| *marron* | Maroon |
| *pain maïs* | cornbread |
| *shak-shak* | maraccas |
| *taro* | a root vegetable |
| *taza* | barracuda |
| *tôline* | tree frog |
| *topi-tambour* | a potato-like vegetable |
| *zodomeh* | a freshwater fish |
| *zouk* | a Caribbean dance and style of music |

## Also in Longman Caribbean Writers

### Consolation

Earl G Long

*Consolation* is a warm, wry novel ... Consolation is a Caribbean village suffering, like so many other villages, the tensions between the old ways and the new, intrusions of Development into familiar ways of living and relating. The publisher's blurb says this is Earl Long's "first published novel": let's hope there are more.

*BWee Beat*

*Consolation* ... is a paradigm of neo-colonialism in the islands of the Eastern Caribbean. Consolation is a village where people fish and make gardens, help and argue with each other through the moments and years of their lives. They are wise in their ways and have no illusions about the self-seeking politicians and their Tweedledee and Tweedledum parties who ingratiate themselves through their village prior to election time.

Long skilfully draws portraits of the village people, lovingly and lyrically describing their village – island – world as a hermetic place where changes come suddenly in the decade of the '70s – "like stones flung without cause or remorse". .

This is a tale of truth, beautifully and evocatively expressed despite all its theme of ugliness and despoliation.

*Morning Star*

ISBN 0582 23913 3

**Caribbean New Voices 1**

compiled and edited by Stewart Brown

This is an anthology of both new and established Caribbean writers, who between them represent islands as diverse as Trinidad, St Lucia, Jamaica, Guyana, Barbados and Montserrat, as well as Belize.

Alecia McKenzie, Jane King, Anthony Kellman, John Gilmore, Terrence Clarke, N D Williams, Christine Craig, David Jackman, Zoila Ellis, Sasenarine Persaud, F B André, Pauline Melville, Jennifer Rahim, Garfield Ellis, Keith Jardim, Ras Michael Jeune, McDonald Dixon and Earl G Long have each contributed a short story, while there is also a selection of poems from Stanley Greaves, Patricia Turnbull, Lawrence Scott, al creighton, Michael Gilkes, Howard Fergus and Judith Hamilton.

ISBN 0582 23702 5

# Other Titles Available

## Longman Caribbean Writers

| | | |
|---|---|---|
| Caribbean New Voices | S Brown (Ed) | 0 582 23702 5 |
| Consolation | E G Long | 0 582 23913 3 |
| Between Two Seasons | I J Boodhoo | 0 582 22869 7 |
| Satellite City | A McKenzie | 0 582 08688 4 |
| Karl and other stories | V Pollard | 0 582 22726 7 |
| Homestretch | V Pollard | 0 582 22732 1 |
| Discoveries | J Wickham | 0 582 21804 7 |
| Chieftain's Carnival | M Anthony | 0 582 21805 5 |
| DreamStories | K Brathwaite | 0 582 09340 6 |
| Arrival of the Snakewoman | O Senior | 0 582 03170 2 |
| Summer Lightning | O Senior | 0 582 78627 4 |
| The Dragon Can't Dance | E Lovelace | 0 582 64231 0 |
| Ways of Sunlight | S Selvon | 0 582 64261 2 |
| The Lonely Londoners | S Selvon | 0 582 64264 7 |
| A Brighter Sun | S Selvon | 0 582 64265 5 |
| Foreday Morning | S Selvon | 0 582 03982 7 |
| In the Castle of my Skin | G Lamming | 0 582 64267 1 |
| My Bones and My Flute | E Mittelholzer | 0 582 78552 9 |
| Black Albino | N Roy | 0 582 78563 4 |
| The Children of Sisyphus | O Patterson | 0 582 78571 5 |
| The Jumbie Bird | I Khan | 0 582 78619 3 |
| Study Guide to The Jumbie Bird | S Gajraj-Maharaj | 0 582 25652 6 |
| Plays for Today | E Hill *et al* | 0 582 78620 7 |
| Old Story Time and Smile Orange | TD Rhone | 0 582 78633 9 |
| Study Guide to Old Story Time | M Morris | 0 582 23703 3 |
| Baby Mother and the King of Swords | L Goodison | 0 582 05492 3 |
| Two Roads to Mount Joyful | E McKenzie | 0 582 07125 9 |
| Voiceprint | S Brown *et al* | 0 582 78629 0 |

# Other Titles Available

## Longman African Writers

| | | |
|---|---|---|
| A Forest of Flowers | K Saro-Wiwa | 0 582 27320 X |
| Sozaboy | K Saro-Wiwa | 0 582 23699 1 |
| The Surrender and Other Stories | Mabel Segun | 0 582 25833 2 |
| Tides | I Okpewho | 0 582 10276 6 |
| Of Men and Ghosts | K Aidoo | 0 582 22871 9 |
| Flowers and Shadows | B Okri | 0 582 03536 8 |
| The Victims | I Okpewho | 0 582 26502 9 |
| Call Me Not a Man | M Matshoba | 0 582 00242 7 |
| The Beggar's Strike | A Sowfall | 0 582 00243 5 |
| Dilemma Of a Ghost/Anowa | A A Aidoo | 0 582 27602 0 |
| Our Sister Killjoy | A A Aidoo | 0 582 00391 1 |
| No Sweetness Here | A A Aidoo | 0 582 26456 1 |
| The Marriage of Anansewa/Edufa | E Sutherland | 0 582 00245 1 |
| Between Two Worlds | M Tlali | 0 582 28764 2 |
| The Children of Soweto | M Mzamane | 0 582 26434 0 |
| A Son Of The Soil | W Katiyo | 0 582 02656 3 |
| The Stillborn | Z Alkali | 0 582 26432 4 |
| The Life of Olaudah Equiano | P Edwards | 0 582 26473 1 |
| Sundiata | D T Niane | 0 582 26475 8 |
| The Last Duty | I Okpewho | 0 582 78535 9 |
| Hungry Flames | M Mzamane | 0 582 78590 1 |
| Scarlet Song | M Ba | 0 582 26455 3 |
| Fools | N Ndebele | 0 582 78621 5 |
| Master and Servant | D Mulwa | 0 582 78632 0 |
| The Park | J Matthews | 0 582 26435 9 |
| Hurricane of Dust | A Djoleto | 0 582 01682 7 |
| Sugarcane With Salt | James Ng'ombe | 0 582 05204 1 |
| Study Guide to 'Scarlet Song' | M Ba | 0 582 21979 5 |

All these titles are available from your local bookseller. For further
information on these titles and study guides available contact your
local Longman agent or Longman International, Longman Group
Limited, Edinburgh Gate, Harlow, Essex, CM20 2JE, England.